Desperate to survive, a cursed witch discovers a bleeding wall and a corrupted valley...

Flames flickered in spots ahead, especially as the sky grew darker. As she approached, Sarena expected to smell cooking or perhaps hear the crackling of wood.

The putrid funk of ancient waste wafted from a bush to her left. She kicked it once, forcing it to fall into the earth. Branches snapped and a dry moan echoed from the dark hole that formed. The wide hole lingered in eternal night, though the morning might gift it with light.

Such a pit had been meant for her or one like her. The sounds within could be the wind as much as a long-rotted body unable to die. Even if she opened the wealth of her power into the pit, all she would do was spend her strength. Any unlife within would carry on, droning beyond the end of time...

Also by Len Berry

Fiction

Vitamin F

Serial Fiction

The Fanged Circle: The Knight

The Fanged Circle: The Witch.

The Fanged Circle: The Assassin

Short Fiction as part of these titles

Dreams of Steam II: Brass and Bolts "Dreams of Freedom"

Gadgets: Dreams of Steam III "Heart of Steel"

Small Town Tales vol. 1 "There Are Always Three Of Them"

Rogue's Gallery "The Mirror of Tila"

The Common Tongue Magazine, Issue 5 "The Choosing"

Art

Elegance

SCARS OF SHADOW

By Len Berry

SCARS OF SHADOW - Complete Edition

ISBN: 979-8-9858100-0-4

Cover Illustration by **Fenix Cover Designs**

Interior illustrations by **Len Berry**

For those Souls waiting for the next challenge to be Borne.

SCARS OF SHADOW

The embers of dusk lay behind a looming wall stained a moist shade of red. Even from the opposite side of the valley, Sarena saw a streak of crimson creeping down the wall like a monstrous raindrop.

In her time within the Northern Keep, she never heard mention of such an unusual place. Smaller walls took decades to build and word of those traveled far and wide. As she traveled, no one she encountered could tell her of such a place. A witch could not hear those she aided.

By herself, Sarena could hear everything. Starving birds pecking at half-dead squirrels. Buzzing insects hunting for pollen.

The closer she walked to the valley, the less the witch heard mewling deer or fluttering butterflies. She was left only with the sound of a dead forest crumbling under her feet.

Dried leaves stuck to the branches of gnarled trees stretching through the valley.

The brown grass under Sarena's boots crunched as she moved toward a collection of flames growing as the day fell into sleep.

No rest would come for Sarena. Her survival demanded she stay lucid and account for the quality of her life. She still had skin, even though it had turned rough and thickened over time. Her black hair stayed in a pair of braided crowns, even though her scalp had a pair of bare patches. Around each bald spot, clumps of the witch's hair defied braiding, the strands too short to stay bound together or uprooted entirely.

She glanced again at the wall. The first streak dried into a ball of rusted red just as another trail sprang from the highest brick.

Sarena assumed the wall had bricks. She hadn't made any of them out, but they might have been small rather than the hulking cubes slaves often pulled into place.

There were no towers on the wall. No torches or sentries. Whatever lied beyond did so in absolute silence. Not even the slightest breeze dared to speak near the wall. Sarena's tongue was far too dry to attempt the task.

Coins still rattled in her pocket, offering salvation to her flesh. Spending them would mean straining her connection to her sisters within the Sanctum. With no one to aid, she could not reap the rewards that lead her to more distant realms. Drawn to the magical salve, Sarena touched one of the coins. Even through a layer of cloth, the ridges on the edge pressed against her thumb, the outline of the Sanctum rose to salute her.

The witch drew her hand away. She wouldn't be able to resist the call forever. If she started to forget again, she would have no choice.

Sarena kept her eyes on the high wall, hoping its secrets would distract her. With night drawing closer, the wall drifted further into shadows.

***

At the beginning of her journey, Sarena walked with two other witches. The trio had been marked by the affliction of unlife, but remained committed to their cause.

Elissa, proud and determined, marched with a bardiche that stood taller than her wide-brimmed hat.

Lila, sweet and idealistic, carried a shield in one hand and a spear in the other.

They followed the foot of the Skyborn Range, though avoided touching the sacred mountains at any cost. Dying was worth avoiding, even in the early days. Risking the Sky Lord's wrath was a useless endeavor.

"It shouldn't take long for us to see the Northern Keep," Lila said.

Sarena laughed.

"We'll get there," Elissa said. "When we do, you can be the first to climb to the top of the tower."

Grinning, Lila walked backward. "Anyone feel like racing to get there?"

After she finished another bout of laughter, Sarena pulled the younger witch close and rubbed the top of her head. "I would—just to let you trip over the hem of your dress, but I've laughed enough for a few minutes."

"I don't know." Elissa shook out her dress, knocking away a layer of dirt from the road. "It might not be a bad idea to see how fast we can go in uniform."

"Really?" Lila faced the path ahead. "We'll go at the same time."

Sarena lined up with the others, shaking her head. Lila practically bounced with anticipation. On the opposite side, Elissa lightly smiled.

Lila looked ahead. "Ready?"

"Yes."

Leaning back as she stretched her arms, Sarena said, "I am."

"Go!"

They dashed down the path, dashing toward the growing day as fast as their feet would take them.

***

Flames flickered in spots ahead, especially as the sky grew darker. As she approached, Sarena expected to smell cooking or perhaps hear the crackling of wood.

The putrid funk of ancient waste wafted from a bush to her left. She kicked it once, forcing it to fall into the earth. Branches snapped and a dry moan echoed from the dark hole that formed. The wide hole lingered in eternal night, though the morning might gift it with light.

Such a pit had been meant for her or one like her. The sounds within could be the wind as much as a long-rotted body unable to die. Even if she opened the wealth of her power into the pit, all she would do was spend her strength. Any unlife within would carry on, droning beyond the end of time.

Green and white blossoms lined the edge of the pit. Such blooms could help her move faster for a short time if she ate the bright leaves before exerting herself. Since there weren't any other patches, Sarena considered the village. Just because she was aware of herself and capable of speech wouldn't save her if the people decided she was a threat. Unlife plagued enough of the population that those not cursed would bait traps with medicinal plants, capturing the most desperate.

Still, even the smallest patch of civilization offered the hope of another gold coin falling from the heavens. Sworn to the aid of others, Sarena needed to find problems she could solve. Helping a child get loose from a tree might offer her a coin. Each token in her purse brought her closer to buying her way back to the Sanctum and salvation from her curse.

A swift thunk struck to her side. She turned to the right, seeing a wooden arrow sticking out of her hip. The shape of a shield spell passed from her mind to the air in front of her.

Two more arrows struck, each cracking the luminous blue of her shield. Her gnarled fingers coiled around her staff before she stepped forward to set loose her own attack.

Her shield shattered. An arrow rushed through the falling shards and jumped into her eye.

***

With each death, the bleak field stretched out before Sarena. There was no color or shadow. Plants avoided her boots. Echoes of small animals scurried across the desolate void.

Claws scratched inside her stomach. Even if she bothered to eat something, the sensation would not fade. No food that touched her mouth offered her the least flavor.

A blister burst on the ball of her left foot. Her elbow creaked as she dragged her staff onward. The knuckles of her right hand swelled, the connected fingers lost color and width. One drop of saliva formed in the back of her mouth before stumbling down her throat, a torture her lips continued to endure.

On the edge of her vision, a pool of pure black lay still. Without light, the ebony liquid refused to offer even a sparkle

"Sarena."

Hearing her name, the witch turned, scanning the void for the voice. She saw nothing save for clump of dying leaves falling through the shadows.

"Who's there?" Her leathery tongue fought to produce the words. Sarena wiped her face, ramming her hand into the wooden bolt still protruding from her eye.

Kneeling at the edge of the pool, the witch dropped her weapon. A pair of shaky hands clutched at the embedded bolt. The weight of her arms pulled on the frayed feathers. Her fingernails scratched through the wood, a few tearing loose from their cuticles.

How far would she go this time? Every time Sarena saw the void of color, she asked herself the same thing. She silently recited the lines of her spells, recalling everything from the slightest sound ward to the widest cannon of power she could conjure. Were there other spells locked in her mind?

Once she'd known how to summon crystal rain from the sky. The central word still escaped her. Or had it been a phrase to call on the latent magic hiding within each cloud? Four times she'd tried to recall the spell within the false embrace of death. Or had it been seven? No matter how much she wanted it, the power was lost.

"Sarena."

Her remaining eye couldn't track who'd spoken to her. She hadn't heard them enough to track where they'd been waiting.

Slipping to her knees, she lay her palms on the ground. Her left hand splashed in the black pool. The fluid slid between her pathetic fingers, unable to provide the bare nourishment of water.

Straightening her fingers, Sarena rested her hand on the surface of the pool. Oily ripples pulsed out, drifting out and fading from view before ever returning. "I ask in death to see the path before me. I ask in life to know the steps behind me."

Her hand turned blue and clear, showing the shadows of ones hiding within her thin muscles. Closing her eyelids, she saw the same haze flood her vision. The outline of her pool remained in place while the rest of the void washed away, not even leaving an outline.

The red-stained wall loomed in the distance, beyond all darkness and void. New globs of blood oozed from the highest bricks, draining onto the surrounding forest. Sarena pushed herself to look within, to see beyond the wall. She saw the beating of a heart, the breathing of lungs. A single voice spoke to her once more, calling her name.

Waves rippled over the liquid surface, vibrating with the tones of her name. Sarena touched the pool with her free hand, reaching into oblivion. When her arm sank deep enough, she felt a spark in her hand. A sudden burst of dull light washed everything from her view.

***

When her eyes adjusted to the light, the void was gone. A purple and orange sky loomed in a circle overhead. Earthen walls surrounded her, each too tall to be climbed, even with the aid of the rotted planks bubbling sludge around her. Rather than linger in the waste, she sat on the remains of other lost travelers. Sarena wondered if any of them were unliving and had forgotten how to return to the world.

The weapons loops in her belt were both empty. Neither of her primary tools rested in the detritus around her.

"Hello." Her voice cracked with gravel. A strain in her neck reminded her of being punched so many times where that body part would stop functioning.

For a moment, she touched her cheek. The dry aged leather had torn when she pulled the bolt free from her skull.

"Is anyone there?"

If someone heard her speak, they chose not to reply.

Stuck waiting, Sarena opened her satchel and checked her belongings. She didn't know where the caestus in her bag came from, but she'd never discarded the fighting glove. Without her main weapons, she had to make due, even if she lacked the strength or training to use such a weapon. Leafy blossoms with jade petals peeked out of a small pouch. A vial rolled against her finger, the contents still glowing with the sticky paste she'd scraped from the body of a moonlit slug.

Further streaks of orange coated the sky while the purple deepened, threatening night. Whoever had thrown her body into the pit didn't care enough to check on her. They'd managed to bind her to the bottom of the filth-ridden chamber, else she would have awakened elsewhere. She scavenged through her satchel again, taking out a small purse of gold coins.

Each flattened disk bore a relief on the back. Sarena touched the engraved domes and columns, brushing the bottom of her thumb against the faint impression of the clouds holding each building up. Only the power of the

Sanctum could accomplish such things. Thanks to Elissa, entry required ten

coins. Sarena hadn't collected that many at one time. They were the only means

she had of restoring her flesh or building a fountain to rejuvenate herself.

"Thought I heard someone." A rough laugh circled the top of the pit.

Grime covered the face of the man staring at her. "Seems this one has some unlife

left in her."

Sarena stood. "As a servant of the Sanctum, I ask for your name."

"Witch, eh?"

"Course she is." Several more dirt-smeared faces lined the edge of the

pit. "Took a staff from her didn't I?"

"Quiet woman. Didn't ask you."

Sarena closed her eyes, wishing for someone to draw her through the

worlds.

"Grown quiet all the sudden?"

She didn't bother looking up. "Sir, I am sworn to aid any who call

upon me."

"You might be a witch now, but you'll turn. They all turn."

"That's why we throw them in the pit. Fancy I might take that pretty

dress off you if we live through this."

Sarena paused. She doubted the woman above her could survive

having her face torn off. The witch's fingers had become tight leather sacks with jagged nails and bone knives poking out at five points. First she needed to find a way to climb out.

Then the witch remembered her vows. Out of habit, she took in a deep breath. "What are you trying to survive? Perhaps I can help."

"I said you'll turn. Doubt you can prove otherwise."

"You're capable enough to get me down here. Why not have me help you until you need me in a pit rather than at your side?"

"You find a way to stop unliving, maybe we'll talk about it."

"But Chaz! I want her pretty dress."

"Quiet."

"What if I gave you the dress now?"

"Can I?"

"No." Chaz spat down the hole. "We're done talking."

The moist glob landed a step away from Sarena's feet. Even with the crud surrounding her, she relaxed knowing the man's insult had missed her.

She pulled out her coin purse, rubbing its sides. Within, the emblems of power clinked against each other, waiting for her to call on them.

***

Somewhere along the way, Sarena had drifted asleep. There were never dreams in her rest, none that she could remember.

Moving her feet, she found mud folding over a stray bone. Puddles lingered around her, carrying the same stench as the pit she passed near the valley. She hoped she was in the village she'd been approaching, though she still had no idea how she would escape.

"Here she is, June."

The woman who'd taunted her before returned, this time with a scrawny young woman missing two front teeth.

"Yeah, girl. That's a nice bit of leather down there."

Sarena didn't wear anything made from the hide of an animal. There were always new ways to insult the condition of her cursed flesh.

Forcing a civil tone, the witch said, "Hello. My name is—"

"Don't care what your dumb name is, leather. Just wanted to see what my sis was going on about so much."

"Why don't you stand up and show her that pretty dress I'm going to pick off your bones."

Despite her level of decay, Sarena lifted a petulant eyebrow. She didn't bother standing up.

"Oh, don't be like that. You'll be dead soon enough anyway."

"Perhaps." She turned her attention to the wall of the pit. A curled root plunged out of the earth, reaching at the bottom of the pit.

A screeching cry bellowed from the distance. The sound pierced Sarena's ears enough for her to clap both hands to the side of her head. She clenched her eyes shut, not wanting any of the high-pitched sound to enter her head through any source. Her fingers twitched more than her degraded hands were accustomed to.

Overhead, the taunting woman fell to her knees. The second woman, June, tumbled over the edge of the pit. Her head bounced along the wall, snapping and twisting with each impact. At the bottom of the pit, June's empty eyes stared down her spine while the muck consumed her.

There'd been no need for either of the annoying women above to collapse. From the expression on June's face, she didn't seem to be in agony at all. Restful sleep lingered over the dead woman's face.

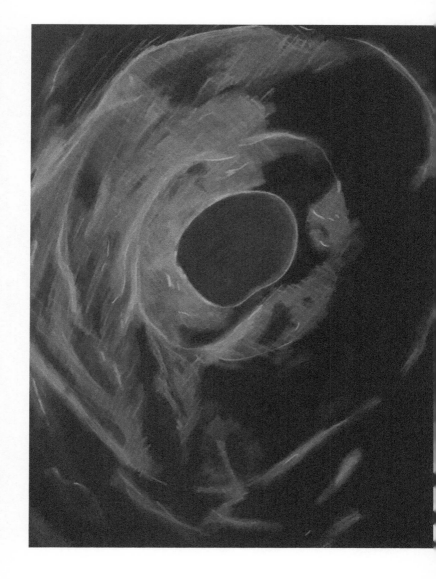

THE PIT

June stank, but Sarena had expected as much. It wasn't the musk of pigs or poultry that dominated many villages. This scent had a lacing of rot, maybe even a fungus.

The witch didn't need to examine June's back to know it didn't have a fanged circle. The dead woman had spoken only with ire toward Sarena, standing beside others as they teased the tormented. The living always turned on the unliving. Even before the curse, people always lied about the dead, disrespecting loyalty, devotion, even what gods the deceased might have prayed to.

Blood gushed from June's neck, stretching into a crimson pool along the side of the pit. Had others not marked by the curse toppled into the pit?

Above, the crass woman who lusted for Sarena's dress lay on the edge of the pit. One arm drooped over the edge, while the bulk of the woman's body rested safely on the firm soil above.

Sarena's soul shook at the thought of being nude in such a discarded place. If it would free her, she knew she would trade her Order's dress if only to part from the village free and intact. Perhaps her sisters had put their dresses aside and turned in their coins. Rumors said Elissa had walked into a dweller nest, but never walked out.

***

Hours passed and Elissa still gazed out from the tower of the Northern Keep. Her wide-brimmed hat lay on a table beside one of the stone walls. She'd loosened her braids so her golden hair could whip in the wind.

"I thought you were the least idealistic of us," Sarena said, sitting at the map table. Ten minutes was all she'd needed to take in her surroundings.

"I'm not sure how long I'll be able to see things like this." The blonde witch turned from the window and gazed at the table. She ran a finger over its surface, touching the carved lines that marked the terrain around the Keep. "Some worlds are savage places."

Sarena laughed. "The last place I went had a pink sky. It was weird."

"Then you haven't seen the worst places."

"Like?"

"Worlds where there is no sky."

"Where it's always night?"

Elissa shook her head. Her ocean-colored eyes glanced up as she spoke. "Where it's always dead."

***

Sarena wished she'd asked what a dead world looked like. She suspected it might look like the dying valley she'd been following. It could easily have a bleeding wall.

She thought of the moment between death and resurrection. Was that a dead world? Would a dead world be worse?

"Stop." Her eyes blinked several times, waking from the nightmare of her own thoughts. Her creaking voice had drawn her back into lucidity, even though she would rather forget her surroundings.

"No. Not that." Forgetting ate at the foundation of her thoughts. She'd already lost one spell from forgetting a single phrase. To forget the slightest thing was to allow more thoughts, more of her innate strength, to fade.

Instead, she turned to the task at hand. Escape.

The pit was too high to climb by hand. Its muddy slopes required a rope to climb, perhaps a pair of climbing hooks. As much as the witch needed to climb out of the pit, she still saw no handholds. There were no tools on hand to climb out, only because the bones on hand didn't look like the could support her weight.

Overhead, the villagers had lost consciousness. Sarena only had two to judge by, but the truth was there. Distant screeching toppled at least two villagers, costing one her life. If the sound killed cretins like June, then it could be a blessing after all.

Unfortunately, Sarena didn't know what the sound was. Where had it come from? As soon as she thought the question, she suspected the answer.

The wall. Something lay beyond. Would it hate her for not falling asleep? Did she have a rescuer waiting to cross the crimson-stained barrier?

Sarena closed her eyes and drifted in contemplation. She hoped a solution would present itself.

***

The scant breath escaping Sarena's lips billowed into a cloud. A dim orange glow crested over the edge of the pit.

Sarena touched one of the rocks that had pelted her skull. Pressing two fingers against her temple made her think of a small opening hidden under a strip of cloth. She hurled the rock, letting it click against the concealed side of the pit.

Bones clattered. The witch looked from side to side, finding nothing.

A low hiss slipped out of the shadows. She closed her fist, unsure of what manner of vermin prowled close to her feet.

One torn glove rose from the muck, held intact with moist detritus and bones. The hand slapped down, grasping a femur. Nearby bones shook like someone was pulling on them, but no one above could have managed the feat.

Another hand snapped over June's chest, spilling mud and rot over her lifeless face. The bony fingers pressed into the villager's bosom, squeezing her to no effect.

"They never checked," Sarena said. Her hip popped as she stood, dropping her against the closest mound of waste and bodies.

"Huu... huu..." The eroded hand clasped June's leg, submerging her body in the true depths of the pit. A brown hood rose from the mire, holding a mud-caked face within. "Nee..."

Sarena cracked her knuckles in an aggressive gesture. Her index finger tumbled loose. "You have got to be kidding me."

"Huu..." The mesh of unliving bodies stood. Amalgamated from at least four corpses, the creature stood on one leg made of two femurs and another made of hands clasped together. His body belonged to an armored knight, though his arms bore the flared sleeves of a sorcerer. "Nee..."

Despite dropping her finger, Sarena shifted into a boxer's pose. Carlton once showed her how to box, but she focused more on the shape of his face, the firmness of his body. Her scant memory was all that could help.

"Huu... Nee..."

"Really? That's what you want?"

The creature scowled as a tube of mud fell from his nose. "Huu! Nee! Huu-Nee! Hu-ney!"

Sarena glanced upward. "You'll have to get out of here for that."

A growl rumbled from the creature's mouth. Then a bark. He lumbered toward Sarena.

She shoved the creature back. He stumbled away from his makeshift legs, falling on his side.

With several plates of armor missing, the witch could see the creature's back. He carried a round scar on his spine, accented with three downward cuts. Every unliving being carried the same mark. There were no exceptions.

Two more hands rose from the pit, dragging their new owners with them. Crafted from the same scattering of corpses, the new arrivals brought with them the same rallying cry. "Huu… nee…"

Sarena hobbled to keep herself between the two. She had no desire to be ripped apart, much less reassembled as some fiend lusting for honey.

The first creature crawled toward her. None of them would ever stop. The curse kept them going just as it left Sarena lingering among the living.

She grabbed a rock, doing the best to ignore the fresh smear of blood on its side. Pushing a grunt from her mouth, Sarena smashed the stone against the closest creature. Bits of wrist bones and powdered muscle dusted the air between them. Spinning, she pounded the rock into the exposed skull of the last aggressor.

With her legs weak from being out of place, Sarena let her weight shift to her knees as she fell on the first creature. The dislocated jaw shifted under her knee, trying either to bite or flee.

Rock in hand, the witch swung down again. She forced the rock into the creature. Every slam pushed it further from unlife into the stoic state of powder and mud. If she thought it would help, Sarena would have set fire to some of the rags.

The other two creatures approached. She hurled the rock at one, then grabbed a stray femur and swung. All she could do was scream as she swung, though the domed end made a decent hammer. Every strike shattered the creatures apart, leaving their bodies further apart and harder to reconstruct.

***

After the sun's light faded from the sky, the top of the pit was as dark as the cosmos beyond. Scattered stars dotted the twilight ceiling, while distant fires made the hole's edge glisten.

The witch didn't move. Her arms locked her on all fours, staring into the refuse of flesh. She couldn't find any sign of June's corpse. With night plunging onward, color drained out of the pit.

Muddy sludge drifted around her fingers and kissed her ankles. A mash of former muscle pressed on her legs and dress with the faintest touch. The amalgamated fiends hungered for the sweetness of her flesh, even though she had also rotted.

Her choice was clear, if only to lure a path out of the pit. Unliving beings would remain prisoner until they twisted into a mindless mass of discarded waste and bones.

She drew one of the gold coins from her purse, holding it between three fingers of her intact hand. The polished edges sparkled, even in the dwindling light. Each engraving stood stronger from the shadows, creating a lifelike visage of the Sanctum. Where the metal touched her fingers, Sarena's hand muscles relaxed and softened, changing shape based on her grip instead of the decay of her body.

Pulling against the draw of the earth, Sarena stood. Her vacant muscles lifted her arm, proving no mass to support the length of her sleeve.

"Sisters hear me." The witch's words choked the decayed bile around her. "From this last bastion of humanity, I beg your help. Infuse me with life once more. Grant me a fleeting chance to enrich the world once more."

If they heard her, the other witches remained silent.

Still Sarena held the coin in offering. It held no value as currency, though she wished it to purchase new flesh. The gleaming emblems could not be saved, only spent in the service of her order.

Gold etchings sparked to life. Light spilled from the disk, washing over the skin of her hand before sinking into her muscles. A fountain of light sprang from her palm and sprinkled over her. Where the light pressed into her skin, she burned for an instant before feeling refreshed. The witch closed her eyes, accepting the renewing shower.

Her first breath drew deep, filling her with excitement and arousal. The orgasmic rush lifted the wrinkles of Sarena's face, gifting her with a smile once more. A neutral tone colored her skin, growing darker in her lips and on the edges of her eyes. Each muscle filled once more. Both pockets of fat grew full and plump as unclaimed fruit. Haze fled from her eyes, showing her firm ridges in the sides of the pit. Thick masses of black hair tumbled over her shoulders until she reached back and started weaving them into braids.

Even as her hands worked through her thickened locks, the witch noticed a shift in the muck around her. She spat the first drop of saliva from her mouth, watching the creatures try to force themselves from a primordial state once more.

Drawing on the light coursing through her body, Sarena turned upward, looking away from the ooze under her feet. "Enlightened Mother, gaze upon this cursed earth. Scorch your enemies within this pit. Instill awe to those who witness upon the surface." Her words evolved into a swooping of sounds, intersecting noises that smoothed an opening in the sky above.

A blinding line fell from the open sky, falling to the depths of the pit. The beam widened, drawing steam from the muck under Sarena's feet. Under the witch, the creatures screamed in half-formed voices as they caught fire. Brilliance washed over the area, reaching beyond the pit.

Empowered even further, Sarena rose from the ground, collapsing close to the lip of the pit. Dry dirt crumbled between her fingers as the light faded.

A dozen villagers stood around the arena, basking in the conclusion to the luminous play. One of them asked, "What was that?"

Thinking of the inherent power of her coins made the witch smile. To strengthen her position, she decided it best to play on the rural fear of divinity.

Sarena stood, brushing the loose dirt from her dress. "That was what happens when the gods look down on us." Holding her hands at her sides, the witch looked from one dirtied face to the next. "Shall we discuss the location of my weapons?"

A ROUTINE OF VIOLENCE

Sarena shifted her eyes from one smudged face to the next. The villagers, so willing to accost her from the shadows, seemed unwilling to move or speak. There were two, maybe three dozen of them, all mired in globs of mud, soot, and occasional streaks of blood.

Flickering torches lit each of their faces, failing to light the dull clubs and plank shields they carried. Among the crowd, someone carried a bow or a crossbow. Did they have enough bolts to fire at the witch again? Would they run the risk of hitting another villager?

Lifting her arms, she took another step away from the pit. "Well? What is it? You wanted me here, at least one of you did. Are you going to tell me or do I have to guess?"

She'd seen shaken desperation several times before. When torches came with it, Sarena had to flee. Civilization did what it could to reject the cursed, lest their unholy affliction spread through the whole populace.

Pointing at the hole behind her, Sarena said, "Two of you spat at me from the top of this pit. Where are they now?" Her fingers craved to peel the flesh off the mouthy woman's face. Her oaths forbade such things. "One of those two wanted my dress, even though it's the only clothing I have."

"They all turn." It was the man from the edge of the pit. Chaz?

"Yet I have not." The witch turned to her left, looking for Chaz among the masses. "I have the blessing of my order. With it, I can rejuvenate myself and build restorative fountains."

Another villager spoke. "And abandon us."

"They abandoned their keep in the South."

"The Northern Keep too."

"Get out of here, witch."

"Throw her back in the pit."

Tightening her fist, Sarena invested a little of her inner strength into her vocal cords. With one forward stomp, she said, "Quiet." Her word shook the ground, pushing the dust away from her feet.

All the villagers stepped back.

"Is this all you have? Ambushes against travelers passing by? Is it?"

Chaz stepped out of the crowd. His shoulders drooped and he kept his head hanging low. "The Catechism says we must purge the cursed from our lands. Then the defilers will flee and leave us in peace."

Catechism? Sarena couldn't recall any such book being taught in the region. "I don't know this text. Who does it say you must pray to?"

A man with gray skin and a blue mohawk emerged from the crowd. His robe once bore a hood, but it had been ripped away long ago. "We pray to Lotac, Prince of the Everlasting Sky."

"Son of the Sky Lord. I have heard of him, but this is the first I've heard of your Catechism."

"The Sky Lord is dead. Iryatha touched him in his sleep. It is said she may even carry his child in the Underworld."

"Folklore." Every village had a story about the Dark Princess who climbed out of the shadows and murdered people with the slightest touch. Unlike the other gods, Sarena never found any evidence that Iryatha was real. "Tell me more of the Catechism. Why is Lotac angry with me?"

"As the unliving grow in number, the crops wither and the soil dies. Water turns to salt and defilers fall from the night."

"And there are defilers here?"

The robed man nodded. "We are all that remains from Siken."

Sarena's limbs went limp and her jaw fell open. "Siken? Surely there are more of you."

"There were three groups," Chaz said. "Defilers come out ever night, try to whittle us down a little more. We've got thirty-three left as of this morning's head count."

"Thirty-three. From a group that was once ten times that number when the original groups merged." The robed man ran his fingers through the azure strands of his mohawk. "The row of refugees I fled with numbered at least a thousand."

Sarena pressed a hand over her mouth. She saw both timidness and fear from the people around her. While it was a familiar sight, she knew the unliving hadn't caused their pain.

In the distance, she noticed the red-stained wall looming over the edge of the valley. She dreaded the answer to her next question. "How far are we from Siken?"

Chaz nodded toward the wall. "It's on the other side of the ridge. Beyond the wall."

"I don't remember Siken having a wall."

"It grew there."

"Grew?" The witch shook her head. "Did the defilers build it?"

"No. It is a defiler. Or many of them. The red is blood dripping down as the old layers die and new levels grow."

"And beyond?"

The robed man turned toward the wall in question. "Those who see do not return."

***

The last wall Sarena confronted loomed in her heart.

Even with her memory torn in places, she still heard the screams.

There had been no coins for her that day.

It was before her back carried any scars, before anyone knew of curses or circles.

She looked toward the Iceblood Gate. Frosted stone spires were her only defense from the legions ahead of her.

One man stood at the front of an army. His sword was too long and cloaked in eternal night. An angry dagger fluttered in his left hand, slicing hands before their weapons could strike him.

He was the first to die. He was the last man on the battlefield.

"Who are you?" Sarena had asked.

Instead of an answer, a sting shot through the center of her back.

***

Beyond the village, an animal howled. Every villager turned away from the witch. Those who had tools held them defensively, gazing at the perimeter of the settlement.

"It's a wolf," Sarena said.

In a soft tone, Chaz said, "The wolves are all dead."

The animal howled again, but let the last sound slither longer than any wolf Sarena had ever encountered.

The woman who'd coveted Sarena's dress marched in a ring, moving from one cluster of villagers to the next. "Get them torches and cudgels together. If one of them bleeds, you boys better burn it."

Sarena approached the robed man with the mohawk. "An attack?"

"Yes. Earlier than usual."

After another twisted howl, Chaz turned around. "If we're lucky, we'll keep them down to one tonight."

Duty pressed down on Sarena. She winced from the strain of her oath, even if it could replace the coin she'd just exhausted. "What can I do to help?"

A high-pitch cry erupted beyond the light of the village.

The mohawked man dropped his robe and drew a pair of long, winding blades. "Protect yourself. Burn them if they bleed."

A dog-sized crab jumped over the villagers, landing on the opposite side of the pit. It had the head of a pig and the mouth of a cobra. Unleashing another cry, it spat at the ground beside the closest cluster of villagers.

Thinking of the general strategy, Sarena screamed. "Don't use—"

One of the villagers swung his torch at the crab. Two lit droplets fell onto the saturated ground.

Sarena expected it to catch fire. She was wrong.

The ground detonated spraying dirt, flames, and bodies in every direction. The witch crouched, blocking her eyes with her left arm. Embers stung the fabric, bouncing off before causing Sarena any real harm. A clump of moist dirt landed where she'd tied her braids into a crown.

Another crab jumped into the village, this one had a bird's head with no feathers. It scurried in a circle on five legs, moving toward Chaz and the mohawked man. Thick slime marked where it took each step.

Sarena reached for her belt and found empty loops where there should be weapons.

The pig-crab spat at a prone villager, then lunged forward with a bite. The bird-crab pecked at the mohawked man, but stayed away from his curved blades.

Four smaller crabs fell into the crowd, all with tall stingers instead of heads. Any capable villagers started swinging at the latest arrivals.

More small crabs drifted out of the sky. Sarena looked up, seeing a faint shape in the darkness. A wide tower shifted like a snake. Faint triangular jaws opened, spewing another batch of crabs landed on the villagers.

"Where are my weapons?"

Chaz ran toward the woman he often bantered with, leaving Sarena with no answer.

A crab pounced on the witch's back, pushing her into the dirt once again. One salty mouthful swirled over her tongue, making her revile the local soil that much more.

Sarena rolled to her left, forcing her body to pin the defiler in place. Cracking rippled under her back. She could feel little limbs scurrying, but they slowed like a clock needing to be wound.

***

Four crabs scrambled after the witch. Her boots kicked loose soil behind her with each step.

To her sides, the villagers fought against the malformed monstrosities. Each creature came coated in a wet sheen, glistening in the moonlight.

Sarena ran toward the most well-built structure in the village, a building with two levels and reinforced wooden walls. If her weapons were anywhere, she suspected—hoped—they might be there.

A crab dug at her heel, missing by an instant. The monster's stinger buried into the soil.

Two of the crabs dashed in front of the witch, blocking her approach.

She jumped, curling into a ball. Midway through the air, her shoulder struck a barrier of wood and worn leather. Her body knocked the door from its setting, leaving both to fall on the floor.

In front of her, she noticed a small fire pit, a futon, and a table covered with ratty scrolls and a pair of books.

Sarena lunged for the fire pit. Sharp thrusts bit into the earthen floor behind her.

Stumbling, she fell onto the table, launching the scrolls throughout the room. One landed in the fire, igniting in a plume of bright green.

A crab leaped onto her face. Another grabbed onto her side.

Leg stalks pricked the skin of her face, digging into her right cheek. Agony ripped through the muscle around her ribs.

A sluggish whimper jutted out of her mouth as she slipped to the floor. Emerald fire grabbed the walls, climbing up to the ceiling. The witch extended her left hand, pushing against the dense layer of air between her and the enchanted flame.

Her eyes drooped. She ran through old commands in her mind. One of them could call fire to her hand or summon the power of a nearby enchantment.

Her eyes saw darkness. Would she forget again? Could she not remember enough to save herself?

Her eyes snapped open.

The crabs scurried away. One crab drooled Sarena's vital fluids as it backed away. It hadn't taken her as they had so willfully kidnapped the villagers.

She shook her head, loosening the paralysis from her eyes. The witch pressed a hand to the wound on her side.

Beyond the smoke, a spire of wood and rope formed a swaying stairwell. Tongues of fire stretched from the closest wall, licking at a few of the ropes holding the steps in place.

Sarena hobbled forward. The skin along her side stretched as she held her wound together. She could feel the torn fibers of muscle hiding inside the sticky hole of her own flesh. Unwilling to leave her wound untended, she grasped one of the higher steps with her free hand as she climbed upward.

Inside her, something shifted, grinding where it shouldn't. Kidney? Liver? She didn't plan to explore to find out for certain.

The ropes holding the steps together swayed. For a moment, the witch stopped, watching as her footing shifted from side to side. Shifted through a sheet of smoke.

Locking her teeth together, Sarena climbed again.

A tense ache crept into her ankles. Her restored body hadn't walked for so long that a natural loss of strength waited for her, even outside of her cursed state. Still, she stepped higher. The only salve waited for her on the next floor.

That was her hope.

More pain surged through her. Smoke rose higher.

Sarena dared to look down just as flames kissed the third step from the bottom.

Rising, she took her hand off the wound in her side. Blood—or worse —slithered down the inside of her dress. The trail wrapped around her leg and touched her gender.

A low growl rumbled in the back of her mouth. She grabbed the floor of the second level just as her eyes began to droop.

Coughing, she threw her upper body into the small upper room. Screams up at her through an open window.

Firelight gleamed through the gaps between floorboards. A thatch ceiling sparked from the pyres outside.

Sarena pulled herself the rest of the way up. A rush of warmth drifted up her dress, heating the soles of her boots.

The walls of the room held up several weapons. Makeshift spears, rusted swords with long and short handles, narrow and wide blades. Her staff leaned in a corner, polished for the first time in ages.

The witch crawled along the floor, feeling the slippery streak of her own fluids as she stretched toward her tool.

Pressing her fingertips onto the shaft, she focused on the things that mattered to her flesh. Heal. Weave. Mend. Her staff let her cheat such things without worrying about the precise mental phrases, though she knew them well.

The phrase to avoid pain eluded her. Sarena screamed from the depths of her diaphragm. Her muscles smashed together, her skin grabbed and clawed for itself. Deep within, her metabolism boiled to make a new slurry of blood. Any aches still lingered since they had no connection to the wounds in her side or on her face.

With a touch of her staff, she knew something more needed to be done. A moment could rally the villagers.

Standing at the window, the witch lifted the staff, filling it with her exhaled breath. Thrusting the head of her weapon forward, Sarena unleashed a screaming pulse, a shockwave of fury left over from an age when gods walked beside men.

Sarena dashed toward the window and jumped, blasting down at a cluster of crabs creeping around the mohawked priest. The light of her magic wrapped around her in a blinding flare.

***

Sarena cried out, feeling the wound in her back. Her hands scrambled to remove the blade, but it had sunk too deep.

She slipped on the snowy field, unable to control her legs. A whimper escaped her lips as she looked up at the cloud-covered keep she'd been tasked with defending.

Far in the sky, the sun blazed with shadow. Its dark intensity grew, plunging the world into the wrong shade of orange and black.

"Elissa." The witch could hardly hear her own voice. "Lila."

A bleeding wall flooded the sky, dripping ichor as rain. Siken lay beyond.

"Wrong," Sarena said. "I was jumping. Crabs were attacking that priest."

The blond witch with the wide hat knelt beside Sarena. "Then answer the question you asked the day you were cursed. 'Who are you?'"

"The last witch."

Elissa tapped her cheek with one finger. "Maybe. If you are, then you can't stop. Pick up your staff and cleanse that village."

***

Sarena lifted her staff. The components of her most recent spells swirled under the surface of her conscious thoughts, hungry as sharks circling a single drop of blood.

Her eyes locked on the towering silhouette, waiting for another burst of smaller crabs to rain from above. A single hair tickled the edge of the witch's left eye. Keeping her gaze in place, her eyelid flickered and the grip around her staff tightened.

Sarena's staff rose only a hand's width from the ground, smashing it back down as she uttered the first line of secret words. Blue trails emerged from the head of the staff, curling to blister the closest three crabs. Each of the pale creatures twitched and flailed, writhing from the impact of each trail

Looking higher, the witch licked her lips as she drew deeper under the surface of her thoughts. A sharp exhale rushed through her nostrils, heating her upper lip. The forgotten sensation almost thrust into the assembling of silent words and inherent commands. The power of each thought cycled in Sarena's thoughts, burrowing upward like an old plow determined not to rust.

She slapped her left hand on her staff, using it to aim her conduit at the looming shape towering outside the village. A single word took shape not only as a spell but as an audible word screaming past the witch's lips. "Oblivion!"

Blinding blue forced every being to turn away from Sarena's attack. Azure light fanned ahead of the staff before a sharp turn raced through the air, fleeing the village before exploding on impact with the defiling shape.

Bits of carapace fell from the beast, each still bathed in an ethereal flame. The silhouette swayed too far back, screaming as it toppled over. It's cry of agony rang not like an animal's death cry, but the wounded heart of a mother watching her children die.

The crabs still within the village ran in circles. One toppled into the pit, another pair collided with each other. The rest fled into the night.

Sarena slipped to her knees, cradling her staff. She propped her forehead on the pole and closed her eyes. Each breath and heartbeat begged for her to wake up somewhere else, away from the damned village around her.

Ahead, the villagers looked at their broken huts and ripped tents. Long channels in the dirt marked where a few of the crabs had taken their prey. A few drops of blood dotted the trails leading away from the fires.

Someone slapped Sarena's back. One finger brushed the fanged circle on her spine. The witch's jaw locked tight and her lips flared open.

"That was some shot, witchy." The woman who wanted her dress, congratulating her no less. "Not bad for one of the damned."

Sarena kept her eyes closed. "You have an odd way of showing thanks."

"Snot my fault you're going to spend eternity in the abyss. If I die, I've got the good sense not to come back."

"It's not a choice."

"Always a choice. Just like how I want that pretty dress after you're gone. You die again, I'll strip it off you myself."

The witch stood, turning toward the desperate woman. "You could have taken it before I was thrown in the pit."

"You were in before I got a look at you." The woman slapped Sarena's arm. "Just stay alive and I won't be able to take it."

A rumbling quake pulled everyone's attention to a low red-orange glow hovering behind the wall surrounding Siken. In the distance, Sarena saw something on top of the wall—a single figure pacing the length of the barrier until the brightest point of light was behind it.

Chaz walked behind his woman and draped an arm over her shoulders. "What you think it means, Bea?"

"Figure somebody over there's real mad."

Sarena nodded, silently agreeing with the woman.

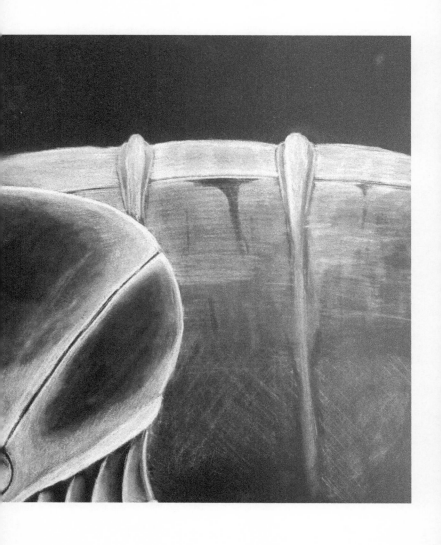

EMISSARY

The villagers took a tally of their number, put out excess fires, and stockpiled weapons. Bea shouted orders easing the others into action.

Sarena kept watching the figure standing on the distant wall. It hadn't moved, especially once the witch decided the village was being watched.

The priest stood next to her, while cleaning blood from his knives. Sheathing his weapons, he asked, "What do you think of our audience?"

"Does he always watch?"

"No." The priest pulled on his robe, then ran his fingers through the height of his blue mohawk. "I've only noticed him a few times. Slaying the worm must have drawn his attention."

"Will that make things worse for you?"

He stayed quiet, gripping the collar of his robe with one hand. "I don't know."

"Does anyone ever pillage from the defilers?"

Trembling, the priest shook his head. "We have enough problems without touching their horrid dead. The only contact we make is dispatching and disposal. We leave the rest to the Sky Lord."

Looking away from the distant figure, Sarena approached the slain worm.

Running after her, the priest asked, "What are you doing?"

"Making use of my curse. Maybe we can get some answers." She didn't care if the villagers approved of her tactics, but if she was being watched, she wanted to know.

Taking a small mace from one of the fallen villagers, Sarena poked the massive worm. Its skin looked reptilian but possessed a firm exoskeleton. A layer of mucus coated the entire worm, the dead substance continued to slip over the monster's curved body.

Without any reaction on the worm's part, the witch struck the fallen beast. The stubbed points on the mace thunked against the walled hide.

Sarena glanced at the wall. The figure refused to move.

"What's wrong?" She held the mace low, pacing around the hulk in front of her. "Aren't you going to do anything?" Sarena swung with the mace again. Having strength in her muscles still surprised her.

As Sarena lashed out, the priest and a few more villagers gathered to watch. The witch glanced at them, but kept her focus on the stained wall and her intended audience.

Grunting, Sarena struck the worm's side. Cracks ripped away from the point of impact. The worm's armored hide flaked apart, crumbling as smaller worms poured out with globs of mucus.

Reeling back, she smashed the mace into the sludge of snot and maggoty larvae. The splatter wrapped around the mace, dripping from it in thick strands.

Sarena stepped away from the mass, hurling the mace at the wall. "What do you want with these people? Is the city not enough for you?"

The figure walked along the wall, approaching a closer vantage point.

Sticking a hand into her coin purse, the witch lifted one of her gold coins. She extended her right arm above her head, holding the bright token with her thumb and index finger. "Do you see this? Do you know what I am?"

A hand pressed on her shoulder. Sarena spun, punching as she turned. Her fist struck the priest, forcing him to the ground.

He held up a single hand. "Peace, fair witch. I do not know if the fiend can hear your words, much less understand them."

She continued staring at the moving figure. "Perhaps not." Sarena turned away, though her gaze lingered.

***

"I hate waiting." Lila stared out from the frost-glazed Keep, waiting for the invaders to come.

Sarena knelt beside her young comrade, looking for anything other than the frozen tomb of winter. "We all have to wait at some point. No one wants to, especially when the coming moment is so terrible."

"It still sucks."

Placing a hand on Lila's back, Sarena said, "Look for one thing and focus on that. Find inspiration in the world around you. There's more here than you think."

Quietly, the younger witch asked, "Do you think so?"

Sarena nodded. "If you can find a way to focus, you'll get through this."

"Unless you want to leave." Both witches turned, hearing Elissa's approach. The tallest witch approached the others. "No one is forcing us to stay. Only our word holds us here."

"And our oath."

Elissa knelt in front of Lila. "An oath is solemn and we should be true, but it is only made of words." She grabbed the younger woman's arm, poking her wrist with a thumbnail. "There is a painful world all around you, Lila. No one can make you stand against it. You have to choose that for yourself."

Lila jerked her arm away. "I'm here, aren't I?"

"Being here isn't enough. So far, you've only said the words."

"Isn't her oath as good as yours?" Sarena asked.

Elissa stood without looking at the others. "It's only words until we are called to act. When that happens, we have to decide if we intend to keep going." She stepped to the edge of the lookout, propping both hands on the long pole of her bardiche. "Once you decide, never look back."

Lila shook her head and walked away.

Whispering with venom, Sarena said, "You don't have to be such a bitch to her."

"It's not her I was trying to convince."

"That was for my benefit?"

"No. Mine."

***

Though she sat close to the largest bonfire, her eyes always found the pit. The wide mouth stayed in place, but the witch could still feel its cold breath. Just because she climbed out didn't mean the stopped hungering for her. Every flash of flame sounded like the panting of a starving dog staring at a nearby piece of meat.

Overhead, the night continued in absolute darkness, a veil beyond black cut only by campfires reflecting on distant clouds. Around the witch, villagers patched their wounds and sharpened weapons of wood and steel.

Bea tied a strip of cloth around her arm. Bands of flame reflected constantly in her eyes. The mud-smeared woman

The priest sat a short distance from Sarena, close enough to seem like he wanted to talk, far enough to scorn one of the cursed.

Still focused on the fire, the witch broke the needless silence. "What sermon did you have prepared today?"

"Dark terrors fill the night. Yet you have not flinched."

"I don't know how long it'll take for him to get here."

"Him?" The priest shook his head. "Who?"

"The man on the wall. He's coming."

"That's absurd. There's no way for him to have seen what happened from that distance. The wall is on the far side of the valley."

Sarena shifted her body toward the priest and leaned forward. "Does your Catechism say anything about the defilers?"

"No—"

"Then you don't know what they're capable of. I don't know either, but my instincts say whoever is on that wall is coming here."

He rose to one knee. "I should warn Bea."

"Wait a moment."

Sitting again, the priest breathed deeply. Frowning, he stared at the ground for a moment before meeting Sarena's gaze.

"Do you still speak for these people?"

"Speak? Y-yes, but it's battle that we prepare for—"

"I can stand with you, fight on your behalf if necessary."

"Why would a cursed woman die for us?"

Sarena reached into her coin purse, releasing one of the gold emblems within. "These tokens are gifts bestowed by my order. I used one to restore myself, so I have seven left. That's seven more times I can restore myself, or I can make three regenerative fountains." She dropped the coin back into her purse. "If I get three more, I can open a doorway to the Sanctum. I can no longer cross the Zenith Bridge."

"Because of the curse?"

"Yes." She pointed in the direction of the massive worm's husk. "If I'd slain that beast in your employ, I would have been given another coin. As it stands, I would leave here right now, but the defilers have changed this entire region. I wouldn't be able to escape them."

"Then what do you suggest?"

The witch took a slim crystal from her satchel. "I write my name with this. You do the same—"

"I can't participate in cursed magic."

"This is the contract of my order, separate from my own power. It's from before the curse took so many of us. With this, I'll be bestowed with more power so long as I stay in your service. This isn't fealty, it's a partnership."

Nodding, the priest held out his hand. "Pass me the crystal."

"What's that?" Bea stood between Sarena and the priest, snatching the crystal from the witch's hand.

"Please be careful with that," Sarena said.

Bea turned the crystal in her hands, tapping on the edge with a fingernail. "You got some fancy trinkets, leather. How'd you manage to get cursed in the first place?"

Sarena pressed her lips shut. Air shoved out through her nostrils. She stared at the filthy woman hard enough that she wished Bea's hair would ignite. "Could you give that back?"

"I ain't hurting it."

"Bea," the priest said, "please. We need that to officially enlist Sarena's help."

"How's that?"

"It's a binding ritual my order uses," the witch said. "I would like that back now."

The filthy woman slapped the crystal against the palm of her hand. Every tap beat out like a bad drummer tripping down a hill. "Doesn't seem right. Cursed gal like you having shiny crystals and a pretty dress."

Sarena stood, holding her fists next to her hips. "The crystal."

"You got that staff and herbs. Why do you need this?"

"Bea, please."

"No way, Armie. You ain't speaking for us no more."

The witch's hand snapped forward, clasping over Bea's wrist. She twisted, forcing her short fingernails into the other woman's flesh. "Let go of my property."

A grunt burst from Bea's throat. She jerked on her arm to pull it away, but Sarena held tighter.

"I am trying to help you, despite every antagonism you throw my way. You wanted my dress, I offered it to you fairly." The witch torqued her grip harder, drawing another wince from the filthy woman. "I fought defilers by your side." She dug her nails in deeper. "You will give my crystal back or I will take it from you. If I have to take it, you will get no further help from me."

Armie jumped to his feet. "Both of you, please. Stop this."

Bea spat in Sarena's eye. The crystal fell into the dirt.

The witch wiped snot and spit off her face, releasing the filthy woman at the same time.

Bea kicked back a puff of dirt as she marched away.

Sarena picked up the crystal, wiping away the dirt. She cradled the rod mournfully, closing her ever-weightier eyes.

"You have the crystal," the priest said. "Shall we continue."

"It won't matter." The witch's voice raised to little more than a whisper. She slipped the crystal back into her satchel. "I need someone who speaks for the village. Your voice is equal to hers or outmatched entirely. There's nothing I can do."

***

The first line of soldiers raced back to the Keep. Those who had enough strength pounded on the gates. Voices moaned to enter.

Sarena stepped away from her post. Squatting on her knees, she wrapped her arms around her calves. Her eyes sealed shut to hold back a watery onslaught.

Lila touched the witch's back. "There was nothing we could do."

"I'll never get over it."

"You'll get your chance." The young witch massaged Sarena's shoulders.

Outside, the wan drumming shook the stone floor and walls.

Elissa looked over the window's edge. "Toxic mists most likely. Half of them are already dead. The others will be by nightfall."

Standing, Sarena threw her staff at the far wall. "Why didn't they listen to us? If they hadn't ran out there—"

"But they did." Elissa marched toward Sarena and locked a hand over each of her shoulders. "All we can do is watch. If they invaders get close enough for us to attack, then we can attack."

"I'm tired of the death."

"Then, when the time comes, do something about it."

***

Standing at the edge of the pit, Sarena glanced into the shadows she once occupied. The amalgamated creatures lingered once more, fused into bodies of refuse and regret.

One of the villagers screamed. "He's gone."

The witch heard Bea talking to the distraught villager. "Who?"

"The man on the wall."

Sarena scanned the length of the wall. The low angry glow still hovered beyond its height, but no one patrolled the top of the barrier.

He'd been watching. He wasn't on the wall.

The witch walked away from the pit, keeping her eyes on the worm-like husk lingering at the edge of the village. She prodded the thick hide with the head of her staff. "You're in there aren't you?"

The worm's jaws unfolded. Threads of sweat and death ran between each of the beast's rudimentary fangs. The shadows within the worm grew darker than those in the pit. Fuligin upon black without any threat of onyx intruding on the procession.

Moist steps paced within the unseeable darkness, though no light moved with them.

Sarena did not speak, though her heart punched her ribs from within her chest. Her left eyelid twitched, straining to blink.

A drone of murmuring flooded behind the witch. "I hear someone in there."

"What's going on?"

"She's just staring in the dark."

The steps stopped. A thud echoed out of the dark.

"What was that?"

Sarena kept her eyes forward and turned her head. "Get back. All of you."

As the villagers shifted back, another thud ripped into the night.

As her heart raced, the witch tightened her grip on her staff, lifting it a hand's width from the ground. "Fill this implement. Touch upon my spirit." A hazy blue glow surrounded the winged emblem at the head of Sarena's staff. The tunnel of flesh and bile shimmered in the faint light. Globs of mucus and semi-digested waste ran down the ribbed walls.

A cracked hole opened a skylight within the worm's necrotic hide. An armored section hung low while a gap of night warped the muscle behind it.

Armie stepped past the witch, staring at the hole. "What's that?"

Sarena lifted her free hand, blocking the priest's path. "Remember what you're standing in."

He looked up. "You killed it."

"There's no reason to think the belly of a dead leviathan can't digest you."

Armie's mouth and eyes dangled open. "I see."

From the village proper, several voices screamed. The crowd that had gathered behind the witch turned and raced back the way they'd came.

***

A wall of mud-stained gawkers spread along the center of the village. Bea shouted with more anger than usual. " —whatever sort of curse you have. Get out of here. Take leather with you."

Sarena scowled since she hadn't been forgotten. The witch pushed further into the village.

A slithering sound curdled in Sarena's ears. Tiny hairs in her arms poked through the sleeves of her dress. The same hairs dug at the skin behind her knee. She tightened her grip on her staff when she saw it shake. When the first audible chill passed, she realized the sounds were words sliding out of an unnerving shadow.

"Bring the one who felled the nydal. She is the only one I will speak with."

The watcher from the wall knew Sarena was a woman. She'd only thought of him as a man because her training told her as much. Women took on few lookout duties, and just as rarely took to the field.

Air filled Sarena's lungs enough where she thought her ribs would burst. She pushed her way through the wall of villagers. "I'm here," she said. If she were on hand, then perhaps she could uphold the vows to her Order one more time.

"Come."

Standing on opposite sides of the pit, the witch stared at the emissary. She'd expected a human, and perhaps he might have been at one time. Segments of scaly armor covered most of his body. Each section shimmered under a coating of the same mucus that covered the massive dead worm. The emissary's pectoral muscles flexed in the night air, shifting the armored segments covering his abdomen and waist. He had no eyes or cheeks, wearing four vented slits in their place. A thick bead of crimson sat in the center of his forehead, leaking down the channel of his nose, lubricating the narrow diamond fold he had in place of a mouth.

A snakelike tendril fluttered out of the diamond slit, bringing about the closest thing the emissary had to speech. "Sister Sarena, Witch of the Sunlit Order."

"I haven't heard your name."

"My name is meaningless. My purpose is nothing."

"Then why are you here?"

"She seeks your mind and the ember that transcends death."

Bea stood up with a knife in hand. She prowled behind the emissary.

"Who is she? The Comtesse of Siken?"

"No, witch. She is beyond your reasoning."

"Then what is it you seek?"

"Souls. Hearts. The essence of all that lives."

"It is customary to ask." Sarena struck the base of her staff against the ground. A clump of dirt fell into the pit. "Your minions have killed or captured many of these people."

The emissary's arms draped to the ground. Snake-like coils swung at his sides, supported by insectile joints. He twisted in a circle, wrapping one limb around Bea's waist. The filthy woman dangled in the air above the pit while the emissary leaned close to her.

Coated in crimson, the emissary's tongue licked Bea's face from one side to another. "These people belong to us. Through them, we shall learn."

A cluster of gleaming orbs burst to life around Sarena. "Free her. Safely."

"You are not bound to her. I heard her shun your crystal and its protection."

Azure radiance spilled from Sarena's eyes and mouth. She pointed her staff at the defiler, filling it with her power. "Release her or I will tear the humanity from your corrupted flesh."

"You are incapable."

The emissary squeezed Bea, drawing a gasping wince out of her.

"You shall burn." The witch thrust forward with her staff, focusing on the assembly of phrases in her mind. Each portion linked together, fusing with the commands that created the orbs hovering around her. She opened her mouth to utter the words that would unleash righteous fury into the defiler's inhuman flesh.

The air remained still. Sparks of illumination around the staff dulled.

Sarena shook her head. The phrase still left its absence in her mind.

The emissary licked Bea once more. "As I said, incapable."

"How?" The word grew as a whisper. "You can't know that."

"It is your kind we seek. The fodder does not matter."

Confined, Bea grimaced at the emissary. "We. Will. Fight."

"Do not spoil your lungs. They are strong enough to breathe for Her."

"You came to speak," Sarena said, "but you've offered nothing."

The emissary withdrew his tongue, exposing a slender diamond with slight flaps around it. "Cease all fighting. When the sun sets a second time from now, strip yourselves, bathe in the saliva of the nydal and eat of its flesh." The tongue emerged once more, pointing at Sarena. "Use your powers to see this is done, then follow yourself. Before the next dawn, you shall all be collected."

Still clutching Bea, the emissary crouched, then jumped upward. Night swallowed him, even though a new day grew in the distance.

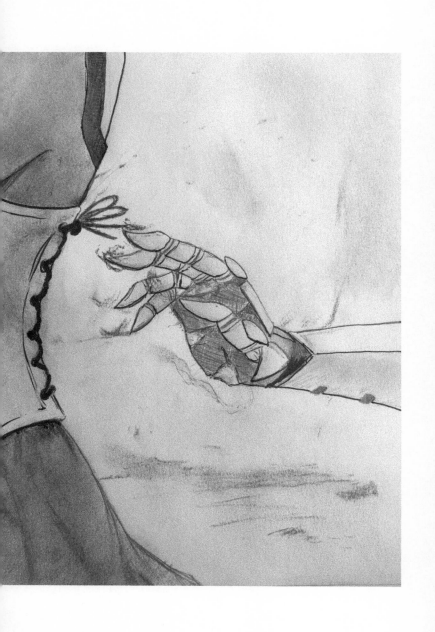

FLEEING INTO THE SUN

Lying on the snow-crusted field of battle, Sarena watched as the shadowy invaders marched through the fallen soldiers. Among the skull-helmed warriors, a lone figure in shimmering onyx touched some of the fallen. A silver helmet with angled filigree covered the mystery woman's face, though crimson hair tumbled over her neck and down her spine.

"Here is another," one of the warriors said, prodding Lila's small body.

The mystery woman knelt, letting the full moon's glow reflect off her armored sleeves and neck. "Barely more than a child." Her voice was seduction and satisfaction. She turned Lila's head one way, then another. "There isn't enough life here."

Black and scarlet smoke rose from the woman's right hand. Extending

her index finger, she pushed against Lila's head. Burned hair and skin crawled

into Sarena's nostrils.

The witch coughed.

An unseen warrior pulled Sarena's arm, forcing her to sit up. "Will you

live?" he asked.

She stared at the mystery woman. "Leave her alone."

"Soon." The woman shoved her finger into Lila's skull, withdrawing it

an instant later. Smoke billowed from the fresh hole. "Your sister?"

"In arms."

"Then you have my condolences. She would not have lived to witness

the dark dawn."

Sarena huffed. A glob of blood burst out of her mouth.

The mystery woman grabbed the witch's face. "There is still fire and

life in you. Answer me this: what would you do to step away from death's

eternal kiss?"

***

Everyone in the village shared their opinion of the emissary's demand.

With every voice speaking at once, Sarena strained under her own thoughts.

Could such a course of action be wise?

The witch approached one of the huts, knocking her staff against the

corner of someone's makeshift home. The wood structure creaked for a moment

under the strain, but the sound cracked through the air. "Everybody, shut up!"

Murmuring fled from Sarena's ears as she scanned the group. Most of them froze, their tools and bludgeons vibrating at their sides.

"You can't—and won't—give in to this. None of you know what that fluid is. Anything could be in that worm's meat."

"We can't keep fighting that," Chaz said. He'd added a gash to his muddied face. "We should run."

"Can you get away from the defilers? Are you rested enough to leave now?" She looked over the thinning crowd again. "It might be the only advantage you'll get if you're going to run. Wait until dawn and it might be too late."

"What do you know?" someone asked her.

The witch shook her head. "I don't know exactly what's going on, but I know the defilers I've seen are fast. Something faster might be waiting behind that wall. Do you want to bet against that?"

Quiet hung over the village.

"I don't think you can get away fast enough. That means you have to do something else."

Armie shifted closer to the witch. "You have something in mind."

The lack of a question pointed the village's desperation at Sarena. The looming silence deferred judgment to the priest, who in turn could call on Sarena for aid.

She drew the crystal stylus from her belt. It lay in her palm as easily as a small pebble. The witch extended her arm. Neither party looked at one another as Armie took the crystal.

He knelt at the witch's feet. No one spoke up. Chaz remained still. Armie pushed the stylus' point into the soil, swooping his hand in patterns to construct his name. The priest elevated the crystal when he finished.

Sarena lifted the stylus and knelt beside the now-singular leader. Her fingers led the crystal through the dirt, leaving swirls of style with her personal title. When she finished, she exhaled, putting the stylus away.

Both names began to glow, with Sarena's gleaming a brilliant gold. The witch touched the scribble Armie placed in the dirt while the priest pressed his hand into the luminescence. Sarena's name faded, taking with it the very marks she'd just made. A glowing circle surrounded the witch, lighting her eyes and skin. The shine continued to grow until she stood. One last flare erased the marks on her skin and the stains on her body.

She bowed to Armie. "I am bound to your success now."

From behind the witch, Chaz asked, "What does that mean?"

Turning, Sarena said, "If your priest were to heal someone, I will also be healed. If I fight for him, it will be as though he did it."

"Are you going to block the defilers so we can escape?" Chaz marched toward the witch. "They took Bea."

The witch punched the man's filthy cheek, dropping him to the ground. "They killed or kidnapped a lot of your people. Have any of you ever gone into Siken looking for them?" She snapped her head to the side, glaring at the other villagers. "Have you?"

Armie's lower lips curled back into his mouth as he shook his head. "We haven't the strength."

"It isn't strength you need," Sarena said. "It's strategy."

Chaz stood up again. His teeth locked together, his lips flared in a snarl. "What do you know about strategy?"

"I know some hothead looking to get back his girlfriend isn't going to last ten minutes inside a city full of defilers." The witch touched her side for a moment, remembering the wound she had there before killing the nydal. "You need unliving fighters."

Murmurs rose among a few of the villagers. Armie stepped behind the witch. "Is this wise? Their belief in the Catechism has already been challenged a great deal with your presence."

"Let them be challenged. If it saves lives, it's the right move."

"And what of their souls?"

"That's between them and the Sky Lord."

Spittle erupted from Chaz's mouth when he spoke again. "You mock our God?"

"No." She could have struck him again, but her hands wouldn't be satisfied with a single punch. "I'm pointing out what I think the defilers will use your people against you in any way possible."

Raising his voice, the priest asked, "Fair witch, what plan do you suggest?"

***

Elissa marched around the perimeter of the Northern Keep, moving counter to the soldiers patrolling the same area. "The mountains give us a defensive wall to the east. On the south, there's not much more than cliffs."

"Which all have fresh wards," Lila said.

Sarena looked beyond the looming keep, finding a wave of dark gray clouds wallowing over the horizon. "The weather makes a curtain of hardship, but we can't count on it."

"Agreed. We'll need to keep an eye on that. There's no telling when the invaders might come."

"Do we know who they are, Elissa? You spoke to the proctor about them—"

The blonde shook her head. "No. So far the only thing that's stopped them has been dismemberment or hurling them into a chasm. Arrows hurt them, but they eventually get back up."

Lila stopped in her tracks. "Is it an army of the dead?"

"Zombies are just legends," Sarena said. "Stories to frighten children."

Without stopping, Elissa said. "Stories are rooted in truth. For every story about dwellers there's a verified account of Iryatha. The key is being able to tell the difference."

Sarena spoke over the blonde's shoulder. "Then what do you

suggest?"

"Try fire. If they get close enough."

***

"Fire." Sarena nodded, sure that she was on the right track. "We burn the city."

One of the villagers fell to his knees, covering his face. "Our home."

"The defilers took Siken from you. If you ever want it back, we have to make it unbearable for them. I'll need a volunteer—"

"Me." Chaz clenched his fists. His eyes stared at the witch like daggers in a fattened calf. "I'm going with you."

"Do you know where I can find flammable materials? What points of the city will catch fire the easiest? Where will one burning building set the rest of the block ablaze?"

Chaz shook his head. "I don't know that. But I'm going."

"You're staying," the witch said. "I'll cut the tendons in your ankles if I have to."

"Bea is in there—"

"Which is why I need a clear head." Sarena turned to Armie. The priest's expression had soured more with each passing minute. "Do you have my answers?"

His voice rose only as a whisper. Had the wind blown, his words would have been lost. "I do."

"Good. We'll need them." The witch faced the rest of the villagers. "Collect what you can carry. Set out before sunrise, if not before first light. Take your fires with you." Only the weakest of the defilers had approached the village's torches. The great worm had kept its distance, though the emissary had stood in the center of the village.

Villagers quietly dispersed to pick up a few supplies. Thrust into the role of refugees again, their sadness could only be seen through the slow steps and the lack of eye contact.

"Is this wise?" Armie asked. "Should we not depart together?"

"No. Someone has to keep the defilers busy while the others escape. If I can buy them a day, it may be enough. If I get lucky, I can buy them two."

"And the third day?"

"Pray the Sky Lord lets us burn the city." With the villagers distracted, Sarena saw her chance. "Do you need anything you don't have on you?"

Wideness shaped Armie's eyes. "My copies of Catechism transcriptions."

"Let's get them. Then we have to leave."

***

As the priest collected his pages, Sarena knelt close to the door of Armie's hut. The witch kept her fists beside her hips as she lowered her head. She prayed where she had trouble hearing her own words. "May the Sanctum preserve me on my journey. May light wash over these people so they might find happier days. May life remain in Armie's heart. May the Sanctum preserve—"

The toe of a boot pushed all the air out of Sarena's lungs. She toppled over her assailant's foot, coughing.

"Trying to sneak off."

Chaz kicked the witch again.

"No." Sarena knew what she meant to say, but heard a gurgle more than a word.

"You don't even know how to get back into Siken. I was in the city guard." Chaz kicked again, but Sarena caught the man's ankle.

A sharp twist of the wrists dropped the dirt-crusted man to the ground. Sarena flipped over, sitting on the man's butt while still locking his foot in place. "I warned you." She took a short blade from her satchel, shoving it into Chaz's ankle. "When I let go, you need to follow the others. It'll hurt for you to walk, but you'll be fine. Pull at this blade and you'll likely slice the tendon in half. Then you'll be the slowest man in the village. Know what happens to the slowest member of a herd?"

The filthy man screamed. "You leather bitch!"

"The slowest member of the herd is the one predators eat. If you don't want to be eaten, I suggest you do as I say." She released him and stood. Dusting herself off, she only bothered saying one last word. "Go."

Chaz walked away, stepping softly on his left foot.

Armie threw open his flap door and emerged from his hut. "What did

Chaz want?"

"Reassurance that we would do our best to help Bea."

"And we will."

The witch said nothing as she walked to the edge of the village.

When he followed, Armie asked, "We will, won't we?"

Sarena didn't look at the priest. "If we can."

***

Sun rose over the valley, casting a steamy gold onto the new day. Patches of scrub and forest dotted each side, turning brown and barren close to the bleeding wall of Siken.

Behind the witch, Sarena could see a string of figures moving away from the village. Quiet words still lingered in her heart. She had yet to grow totally cold, even toward a public that had cast her into a pit for the cursed.

Armie scratched his blue mohawk. "I don't know if the defilers would have left the central gate intact."

"From the direction I first entered this valley, I should have seen the gate when I first entered."

"And you didn't. Where does that leave us?"

"In need of a key."

"Which we don't have."

Sarena smiled. "Actually, we do." She lifted her staff. Sunlight caught the tip of the blunted eagle shape where she channeled the bulk of her power.

"You mean to blast through the wall?"

"In a manner of speaking. Was the pit you threw me in the only one?"

"I didn't throw you in the pit."

"Fine. Bea and Chaz. The villagers. Whoever. Is it the only one?"

Armie frowned, looking over the landscape. "No."

"Good, then we'll have help."

"Help? But the Catechism forbids engaging the cursed for any reason aside from purification."

Sarena shifted her shoulders. The fanged circle tingled on her back. "I think I'm still cursed."

"But you purified yourself."

"Stab me to death and I'll wake up in that pit." The witch raised one hand in defense. "Please don't do that. Still, if I'm killed, I won't stay dead. I'll end up a little rotted in the pit. It's where I'm currently bound."

"Then why seek another one?"

"Because there might be someone else cursed and unable to get out." The witch tapped her side, unable to feel where the defiler pierced her flesh. "I got a nasty wound from one of those crabs, the ones that kidnapped a few of your people. It let go of me."

"Perhaps it didn't sting you as deep as the others."

"It made a hole as big as my hand. Blood, pee, and everything in between was leaking out of me."

Armie's face became slightly pale. "Sounds putrid."

"I was too busy not dying to notice." Sarena squeezed the bridge of her nose. "My point is that the defilers got a solid taste of me and spat me back out. I'm hoping that means they don't want anyone who is cursed."

The priest raised a finger next to his face. "And you want reinforcements."

A subtle smile rose from Sarena's mouth. "Yes."

Moving his finger downward, Armie pointed at a shadowy crevasse. "The first pits we built were in there. Tests to see if they could trap…" His head hung low. "The cursed."

The witch didn't bother correcting him. She knew what he'd intended to say. The fact that he felt any shame made Sarena feel like she had a chance at dealing with the general population. "Did anyone ever check the pits?"

"At first. Then we started laying them as traps throughout the valley."

"So anyone could be in there."

"Or no one."

She didn't bother with a response. It would do nothing to raise morale. "Let's go."

***

Dead torches lined the edge of the crevasse. Sunlight beat its way into the crack, overflowing into a blinding beam.

Petrified boards blocked Sarena's boots from touching bare rock, though pastel flowers jumped through the gaps. Rusted swords and broken staves lay in pile covered by loose dirt and cave drippings. A dulled whine puffed from the shadows ahead.

Armie issued a low whisper. "Someone's in there."

"But are they still sane?" Sarena walked deeper into the crevasse, never letting her staff touch the ground. She walked on her toes, though she didn't expect any echoes from her boots. Anything could be waiting, not simply one of the cursed.

Standing at the mouth of another pit, she looked down. Shadows lingered around her, pouring into a deeper shade of eternal darkness. The whine rose from under her feet.

The witch kicked over a bit of soil, waiting for it to sprinkle below. Someone coughed, though it wasn't Sarena or her companion. She looked at the priest only to find eyes gaping with shock.

"Hello?" Sarena waited for her echo to fade. "My name is Sarena. I'm a —"

"Keep. Quiet." A voice from the pit.

She lowered her tone to a whisper. "I've come to help—"

Sloshing and clanking rumbled from the pit. "Dammit lady." A deep groan followed an angry clatter. "I wish you had a torch."

A thick impact sloshed the unseen muck below. More thrashes tossed soil, water, and unseen collections of mass and forgotten lives.

The witch shut her eyes and took three short breaths. Not bothering with whispers, she asked, "How many of you are down there?"

"All of them. Throw me a torch or get me out of here." An empty huff broke up the man's response. "Help me or get out of here."

Sarena snapped around. Armie stood entirely in the light, never venturing into the shadows of the crevasse. "How many are down there?"

The priest trembled. "I don't know. We never counted."

"How deep are these pits?"

"Another house lower in the earth. We didn't know."

"Damn it. Get some rope." She knelt at the edge of the pit. Squinting, she could see one figure thrashing at something else, a shape she couldn't identify. "Pits." Sarena raised her voice. "Hold them off. I'm going to try something."

The witch focused deep in her mind. Her thoughts swirled, trying to block the ascension of the phrases she sought. Screams of burning soldiers filled her head. Ash-crusted arms flailed. Cries dried as roaring plumes of flame ate through their throats and mouths. Sarena tilted her staff into the pit, willing her thoughts of fire out of her arms and through the magical conduit.

A blazing triangle reached down, piercing through the amorphous glob of organs and discarded death. The witch screamed, her fury acting as further kindling for her scorching wave.

Six voices begged without words. Makeshift arms reached up, begging the witch to stop.

Only when the arms collapsed did Sarena consider stopping. Only when the amorphous glob became crusted with warm ash did she restrain herself.

Below, she heard a brief response. "And I thought I was mad."

***

Armie returned to the crevasse after the amalgamation kindled for some time. He drug a worn coil of rope that draped over his right shoulder. "Where do you want it?"

Sarena pointed to the edge of the pit. Tongues of fire lit the opposite base of the putrid hole. A smoky cloud of cooked rot drifted along the low ceiling of the crevasse, refusing to scatter to the wind.

"Got it." Even out of battle, the man's voice sounded low and empty.

The witch watched the rope pull tight. Both men held their ends as the captive worked his way up the wall of the pit.

A dried sleeve of studded leather slapped the surface. Sarena knelt, grabbing the captive's arm. A hand of sinew and bone locked around her elbow. The thumb's front ridge pushed into the sleeve of Sarena's dress, biting the skin underneath. Wincing, the witch pulled back, trying to get the man fully out of the pit.

Two beady eyes, barely more than lenses locked in balls of waste, locked onto Armie's mohawk. "Priest."

"Yes." Armie clasped his hands over his knees. Each of his lungs gasped for air. "Blessings of the Sky to you and—"

The man swung, knocking Armie back with a full set of sharpened knuckles.

The priest scurried back on his elbows, unable to stand. His attacker shuffled closer.

Sarena slammed the base of her staff against the floor. "Stop this."

In the village, she'd been called leather. Without a mirror, there was no way for her to know if she had ever looked as dried out as the face that turned toward her. Cracked lips parted, exposing his tongue a second time along with the hole in his cheek. A groan curled from deep inside the cursed man. Sarena eventually realized it had been a word. "No."

Armie scurried to his feet, pulling out one of his daggers. The sunny day glimmered off the weapon's edge.

"You pray to Sky." The cursed man shambled onward. "You die."

The priest reeled back. His wave-shaped blade swept forward, crashing against Sarena's staff.

She stepped between the men. "Kill him and we'll have to do this again. We need him."

"He's gone mad already."

Sarena bit her lower lip. "Those lost to the curse don't speak. Do they?"

The cursed man struggled against a tension in his neck. A spurt of mud fell from his shoulders. Slow, he shook his head. "Not. Lost."

"Angry." The witch nodded. A weight of water flooded the bottom of her eyes, but she closed them so nothing would escape. Her fingers drifted into her coin purse, drawing out a single gold coin. "Let me restore you, brother, so you might rise again."

"Are you mad?" Armie asked, peering over her shoulder. "You need those."

"We need him more." She lay the coin in the palm of her hand and extended it to the cursed man. "Take it. Clasp it tight."

He stared at the witch until her heart ached. She'd felt the hurt in the mounds that acted as his eyes. If she'd still been in the village pit, Sarena wondered if she would have already gone mad. Some of the cursed only took a few deaths to lose themselves. Others managed to endure almost to a level of skeletal rot, though she'd never seen it.

The same rugged hand that wounded the witch's arm reached for her hand once again. The rough fingers hovered over the coin. Golden sparks rose from the emblem, making the man's tendons flex. With two fingers, he swept the coin from Sarena's hand, trapping the light within his fist.

BLOOD ON THE SWAMP

Restored, the dark man approached the edge of the crevasse, shielding his eyes from the light. He breathed deep, stretching his arms until both of his elbows popped. Smiling, he took in a deep breath. "Ah, the sweet smell of summer."

Armie followed the man, though stayed several paces back. "May the blessings of the Sky warm your days and brighten your nights."

The man turned, frowning. An instant later, a smile sprang back onto his expression. "Yes, the priest. I suppose you seek apologies for trying to kill you before."

"No." The priest shook his head. "I blame the curse."

"I don't. Men and women with blue mohawks tossed me into that pit and I doubt they ever planned to set me loose."

Sarena stayed back, watching her companions. They were a necessity for what she had planned. Her efforts to help others pushed onto her shoulders, straining her joints. "We need to find others who are cursed. Aren't there other pits—"

The restored captive held his hand up. "Don't bother. Anyone else in those pits has been chewed to dust. All that's left of them is that conglomerated soup you saw at the bottom."

"Such a fiend was in the bottom of my village's pit as well," Armie said.

The man raised an eyebrow. "And how did those people get there?"

"It doesn't matter," Sarena said. "We need to get into Siken."

"I suppose you expect to enlist my aid for that."

"You can burn every house in the city if you like."

"But? The scrolls. Bea."

"That's secondary," the witch said. "We have to strike the defilers while we can."

The life washed from the restored man's face. "Defilers?"

"Fiends that fuse with local life to make unholy monstrosities."

"Insect armor but reptilian skin?" The restored man said. "Fluid on their bodies, not slime, not saliva?"

In an empty gasp, Armie said, "Yes."

"You've seen them," the witch said as she stepped into the opening of the crevasse.

"In Loric and in South Reach." No joy sparked in the man's face, no passion in his movements. "They're spreading along the coasts and crawling inland. I came here to see if Siken would help."

The priest slouched to his knees. "If we had only listened."

"Your city would still be here? You wouldn't have needed to watch hundreds of people die? I heard the story from several priests on my way here. It's grown quite droll."

Sarena put a hand on Armie's shoulder before addressing the restored man. "I mean to fight back. Will you help us?"

"You say they're still in the city?"

"Yes. They send attackers into a village of refugees when night falls."

"First I'll need to find Night's Edge. Then I can help you."

The name lingered on Sarena's tongue like a familiar song whose title had been lost. "Who was that?" she vacantly whispered.

"Another cursed indeed." The restored man snapped the heels of his boots together and crossed his right arm over his stomach. "I am Joseph Armand, lead raider, Legion of Flame."

The priest perked up from the ground. "The Legion of Flame."

"Yes, that is what I said. Why do people always feel the need to repeat the title of my company?"

Armie extended his hand. "Sir, please, I would be honored…"

Joseph took the priest's hand, shaking it for a second at most. "Yes. The honor is mine. Pleasantries and so-forth. Now, my sword?"

"I saw a pile of weapons over there." Sarena pointed to the mound of wood, canvas, and rust.

Flaring out his hands, the raider marched toward the pile. "Really? Night's Edge was left in this pile of dust?" He pushed against the pile with the toe of tailored boots. "Despicable, these priests, how they treat such weapons."

Sarena recalled the cache of swords and staves she'd seen in the village. Were any of them renowned weapons?

Joseph crouched, scouring through the pile. "There are five swords here for every bloody idiot they threw in that pit."

"I'm sorry, Legionnaire." Armie shook his head. "I—"

"Didn't know. Yes, yes. Make all your excuses, but you're the only one here I can blame."

The priest's jaw dangled open.

Sarena tapped him on the shoulder as the raider continued to scavenge. "Is there a chance any other weapons would be nearby? Most of those are rusted."

"There's nowhere else. Cursed fiends carry cursed weapons. The metal cannot be reforged, nor can we risk their owners being armed."

A curl pulled down the edge of the witch's mouth. At least Armie hadn't called her "leather."

"Here!" Joseph pulled a long handle from the mountain of armaments. As he lifted the attached sword, the cutting edge glimmered, though the rest of the blade cast a constant shadow. The raider turned the sword over, examining the sides of his weapon. "Such poor treatment for such a fine weapon."

Armie lowered his head. "My most solemn apologies."

"Elaborate later, priest. For now, we'd best be to our task. Right, Sun Maiden?"

Sarena glanced to her sides, expecting to find someone else nearby. She only knew Sun Maidens to be active priestesses within the Sanctum. Traveling away from her Order, she'd forgotten the term existed or that it could apply to her. "Yes. Time is not our friend."

They all walked from the crevasse, Joseph, Armie, and the witch following behind.

When sunlight touched Night's Edge, its onyx surface gleamed with a greater darkness. Sarena tasted metal in the back of her mouth, enough that she wanted to gag, but was unable.

***

The trio circled the defiled wall surrounding Siken. No emissary walked its surface, though crimson beads still dribbled from its seams.

Joseph gazed at the wall whenever he was sure of his steps. "I've never seen anything like that."

"Even with as many places you saw overrun with defilers?"

"Not even then, Sun Maiden. I've crossed this entire continent since I left my father's foundry. Priest, I'm sure it surprises you that I had a meager youth."

Armie said, "No. Many called to glory come from meager beginnings."

"Not in my experience. Most men who have common origins end up leading meager lives. Nobles and clergy tend to shun greatness rather than excel beyond what they are."

"An enlightening perspective." Sarena couldn't recall meeting anyone from the Legion of Flame. If she had, she doubted they shared Joseph's views, much less the willingness to voice them.

***

The day wore on in near silence. Armie's deference held any questions in check. Sarena didn't want to provoke Joseph's tongue, at least not to speak. The witch avoided looking at the wall, instead favoring the Legionnaire's backside.

The priest lifted a finger. "There looks to be more leaking from that section of the wall."

"Sewers?"

"Maybe," Armie said. "We'll have to cross a bog or go around if we want to look."

Under the shadow of the wall, a wide marsh crept over the valley. Gnarled, leafless trees reached out of the muddy, red-tinged soup. Thin grasses and reeds stirred the surface of the dark water. Tiny animal songs broke the murky scene.

"How wide is the swamp?" Joseph asked.

"Not sure."

Sarena nodded. "Then we need to cross."

The Legionnaire grinned. "I don't suppose you were hoping for a reason to undress just for me."

Pulling her dress over her head, the witch said, "If I was, we'd have to wait before doing anything about it."

"Right. City to destroy and all that. This is what the Legion of Flame excels at."

Joseph's statement thrust a chill into Sarena's skin. The cool sensation eclipsed the exposure from wearing only a modest bodice and underleggings.

Armie removed his robe and coiled it around his shoulders. Joseph rested his blade over his shoulders, not bothering to remove any of his gear.

"I thought you'd be more protective of your sword," Sarena said.

"And I thought you weren't going to offer me a view of that wonderful creamy skin." The Legionnaire paced around the witch. A smirk slithered over his face. His eyes swept up and down. His lips twitched with every gaze of Sarena's curves. "Very nice indeed. Pity the Princess kissed your back. You would be truly flawless indeed."

Sarena took a deep breath. Her fingers craved to reach into her hair and pull loose her braids. Her hands could remove her remaining undergarments in seconds. She looked away from Joseph and stepped toward the swamp. "It'll have to wait."

The priest shifted his belt of knives. "Coming?"

"Of course," Joseph said. "I never thought I would be so eager to have cream in my coffee."

Calling back, the witch said, "I heard that."

"Of course you did, darling. One must have goals beyond fire and murder."

***

The swamp proved warmer than Sarena expected. Mud around her legs massaged and soothed her muscles. Opaque water refused to fight her joints. With her gear bundled into her dress and tied behind her shoulders, the witch held only her staff. The head of her implement aimed forward, presumably in the direction of the edge of the marshes.

Enough gnarled trees reached out of the bog to block Siken's wall from view.

"I find this entire area far from relaxing." The Legionnaire brought up the rear, likely for the purpose of serving his own eyes. "Dreary, soggy, wet in all the wrong ways."

"You could have stripped your gear." Sarena hoped Joseph's scar didn't blemish his skin.

"As much as that would satisfy you, I would end up even soggier. At least the swamp isn't acidic."

"Please don't tempt fate, esteemed friend."

"Friend? How forgiving of you, priest. I hadn't suspected you wanted to spend the night with me as well."

"I-I didn't—"

Joseph bellowed with laughter. "I haven't enjoyed myself this much since the legion shattered."

"How did it happen? I've only heard stories."

Sarena didn't interject. With the Legion of Flame disbanded, there was no single force ready to patrol the realms. Only the witch and her sisters could cross the veils to protect those in need.

"It is always study and scholar with you, priest? Eventually, you need to look up and tell Lotac to give you a day off."

"Sacrilege."

"But truth. What good is a priest if he doesn't know when to tell the gods to sod off?"

The idea pleased Sarena. If she ended up in the presence of even a lesser god, would she be able to voice her thoughts? Or would she cower like a beggar, praying for a scrap from the table?

"I'm surprised you haven't bothered our Sun Maiden for tales of divinity. She has enough coins to buy multiple doors to the Sanctum."

Her stride slowed. Joseph knew the past but knew nothing of the modern rules, especially not The Final Edict. "The price has gone up. One is no longer enough."

"So the Sanctum fears the curse as well."

"Enough to pay dweller slaves who kill." Sarena hated saying it, but admission was key to coping. "They have thrown dark coins into the world as well."

"Payment for thieves and murderers, I assume. But would the toll open the Sanctum or another door?"

"I don't know. I have never seen what the assassins seek to gain." Sarena hoped such dark-souled people weren't being admitted into the Sanctum. Mindless killers had no place in the realm of rational beings.

Dots of light twinkled over the surface of the water. A few lingered in warm colors, a few dabbled with cooler hues. Each spark moved about on its own, though they all drifted ahead of Sarena at some point.

Softly, Armie said, "The wisps seem curious."

"I've never known a wisp to be curious," the Legionnaire said. "Most of them drift around looking for pellets to feed on."

Sarena thought of sparking her power in an arc. Remembering the loss of the central phrase, she shook her head. "This isn't right."

A wisp drifted to the left of the trio, its body shaped like a small boy with chubby cheeks.

"I've never bothered dealing with fat children. Unless they were fans."

The witch groaned. "I can't decide if you're a fighter or a fame-addict."

"Who said I couldn't be both?"

Three wisps lined up in front of Sarena, all swaying between green, blue, and red. Sometimes together, sometimes as a pair with an outlier.

Imbue. That's what her soul screamed. A crawling sensation in her diaphragm begged her over and over.

The witch stopped and turned. "Armie, your blades." Sarena filled her staff with a pale blue hue. "Draw them."

Nodding, the priest did as he was told. Sarena passed her staff over the weapons, washing them with the light azure glow.

"Imbuing weapons? Don't you think that's excessive?"

"A hunch. Want me to do your sword?"

"Night's Edge doesn't want your spell." Several wisps buzzed overhead. The three ahead strobed with changes in their light. "Even if I wanted it."

Three more wisps bunched together on each side of the travelers, making nine in total. The same colors passed through each. Chubbiness drained from their faces as they grew in size and maturity. All flew within their auras, while their smaller kin continued to buzz around randomly. Together, the nine lifted jagged ethereal daggers in their right hands. They snarled and opened their mouths.

With one scream, they lunged forward.

Sarena blasted at the first trio, though her magic passed through the wisps like a soft breeze moving past tall grass.

Armie thrust at one of the wisps. His blade pierced through the wisp without it noticing.

Night's Edge swept to each side of the group, dropping at least one wisp with each stroke. Everything paused.

"What? Don't you know what 'Princess-kissed' means for a weapon?"

The Legionnaire jumped from the water, practically flying from the use of his legs alone. A flurry of wisps raced toward him, falling moments later as a rainbow of sparks sizzling in the swamp water. "Forward," Joseph said. "Move. Now."

He stomped through the thigh-high muck, splashing a path outward with his speed. Night's Edge slashed through the air, screaming as it ripped through the tiny astral forms and their larger brethren.

An ethereal dagger bit into Sarena's leg. The wisp rose from the swamp water, grinning. Giggling. It stabbed her again.

Armie thrust his blades through the wisp. Others started giggling too.

"I said move."

The priest snapped forward. "Sarena's hit."

"Damn. We don't have time for this." Joseph attacked one of the trees, felling it in one stroke. The gnarled timber splashed into the swamp, sending waves in two directions.

The Legionnaire shifted back, extending a hand to Sarena.

Bile lingered at the back of the witch's throat. She took the man's hand.

"In a moment, you'll be able to attack them," Joseph said. He pulled the witch up, dragging her forward. "We do not want to be here when that happens."

The Legionnaire pointed at the felled tree with Night's Edge. The ebony tip gleamed with hunger and lust.

***

On a field of snow and violence, Sarena summoned an arc of blinding blue spheres. Each of the thirteen dots moved in formation above the crown of her head.

To her left, Elissa spoke the Name Of The Gods. A golden sphere burst out around her. The unliving soldiers blasted in every direction. Two of them went spiraling through the air.

Lila spun her staff, coiling arcs of sapphire all around her body. She thrust the head of her weapon at a man in thick armor. A torpedo of light ripped through the body and the soldiers following.

Beside the youngest witch, a blur of motion jumped through her defenses. All Sarena could see was a black blade, dripping with death, aching for more.

***

Onyx continued shining in the light. The witch focused on Joseph's weapon as it warded the wisps from approaching.

Behind and above them, to the sides, the glowing entities still giggled. Sarena drew up her staff, filling it with another wave of her power.

"Do save your strength," the Legionnaire said. "You'll know when you can wound the wisps."

Every time she blinked, Sarena's eyes felt sticky. Her eyelids threatened to adhere to her cheeks and never let go. When did wisps become so violent?

"Keep your eyes open," Armie said. He pressed the back of his hand against her shoulder. If he hadn't been carrying two blades, it would have been the palm of his hand.

She blasted one of the twisted tree branches sticking out of the water. Rather than using a gleaming blue spray of magic, the witch cast simple flames upon the felled wood.

Every giggle stopped, bursting into a hiss.

Joseph shifted to put both hands on his sword. "We're about to have a serious problem."

Sarena braced her hand on the Legionnaire's back, pulling deeper on her lungs to take in a simple breath.

The auras around the wisps dimmed, though their color remained bright. Tendrils whipped the surface of the water, connecting each gleaming spirit to a shadowy mound under the surface of the swamp. Clustered hisses shifted away from being a gathering of individuals.

A large reptile's head burst out of the shadow, roaring in defiance. Tusks curled up from its eyes. The longest, sharpest of the reptile's teeth whipped out on a tendril, glowing almost as bright as the wisps.

Armie stomped to the witch's right, holding both curved daggers ready. The magic endowed to both weapons still lit the widest band of each curve.

Sarena tried to stare through the wide mouth growling ahead of her. If she could lock her eyes open, if she could look through the swamp beast, then her magic might penetrate the creature's flesh.

The Legionnaire made another jump in the air. Such a great leap came with a slash of black tearing through the cords of skin bonding the wisps to the beast behind them. Joseph came down with a battle cry echoing from the back of his throat. The beast snapped at him, but he jumped back, practically ignoring the water around his legs.

"Fight now! Strike."

The many-tusked mouth lunged at Joseph. The Legionnaire jumped back again.

Sarena released all her unspent fury. Her eyes widened and her lips flared away from her teeth. Each of her fingers coiled around the shaft of her staff, bracing it as brilliant blue rushed into the damp air. The witch cried out in rage. The ache of the wound in her leg threatened to overtake her. Moisture splashed out of her eyes, not tears, but an overflow of sensation.

All around them, wisps screamed, buzzing away from the bright blast. Most of the color winked out of the swamp. The only remaining shades were deep greens and the most blinding waves of blue.

The swamp beast flailed its feet, thrashing water every direction. Its projected tusks and the attached wisps whirled around in frantic vortexes. Tongues of blue flame lingered on the edges of the canal carved by Sarena's blast.

But the tusks stilled, the wisps stopped whipping. Again, the beast shifted toward Sarena and Joseph.

One shout of effort curled through the air. A pair of suddenly-blinding curved blades shredded the air before piercing the beast's armored hide. The monster released a high-pitched whimper and flopped into the water.

Armie climbed the beast's head. At the top, he lifted both blades over his head. He suddenly knelt, shooting both tips into the large monster once again.

If the swamp beast ever breathed, it stopped, never to start again.

No wisps flew out, for they all died with their master. The larger wisps bobbed along the surface, grasping to the knives connected to their backs and long coils extending from the beast's mouth.

Sarena stumbled forward, unwilling to let her head slip below the murky surface. Her lungs itched from the inside. "What was that?"

The Legionnaire rested Night's Edge on top of his right shoulder.

"Some variety of defiled beast from the look of it. The smell's terrible too."

"The wisps?"

"Co-opted," Armie said. The priest ripped his blades from the beast's skull and sheathed them. "I think they were forcibly fused to this creature for some malicious purpose."

The witch leaned half of her mass on her staff. "Then we must keep moving." Her eyes hung low as she walked, threatening to close.

NIGHT'S EDGE

Sarena's feet grew heavy from the swamp burrowing between her toes. It hadn't been much at first, but as she moved under the leafy canopy, more muck stuck between her toes. She didn't remember if her boots were on her feet or rolled within her dress. A pair of shoes grew over her feet, shoes she'd never seen.

Around her, the smell of acid and rot drifted on the surface of the water. Layers of crimson skin congealed in spots within the wide pool. When the spots became long bands and refused to break, the witch heard Joseph speak.

"I can see the shore up ahead."

Further back, the priest asked, "Is it safe to disturb those red patches?"

"If you like, I'll go first. Call it a demonstration of my goodwill."

Sarena shook her head. "If we die… The pit…"

"No need to worry." The Legionnaire's wide mouth smiled. "I'm more resourceful than you might expect."

Armie let Sarena rest against his weight. The priest put an arm around her roll and shoulders, helping her to stand taller.

Joseph extended his onyx blade, half of the length hovered over a band of crimson skin. "I pray this won't scar you, old friend." Grasping the hilt with both hands, the Legionnaire swung downward. Night's Edge struck the deep red band without penetrating the water.

A perfect line trimmed the band in half. Current let the halves drift away from one another.

The priest loosened his grasp on Sarena's shoulders. "Such precision. We are lucky to have such a skilled ally."

Sarena said nothing, only tasting metal in the back of her throat.

***

After the Legion departed, the Northern Keep became a pyre in defiance of the Sky Lord. Once-pristine stones had charred brown and black in flames left by the unliving hordes who'd attacked.

Sarena could taste the stinging of her neck.

"Hold still," Elissa said. "I know it hurts, but I'm almost done."

The witch's face hung low in her sorrow. Her eyes glared up, fueled by a newfound hate.

Cracks of flame burst through the courtyard. A mighty blaze lifted behind the Keep's great stone archway.

"There are more of them now. Cursed to feel true pain without any escape. I feel the mark on my back the same as I'm sure you do. But we can't stop. Our oaths mean more than a curse thrown at us."

The first words of unlife creaked out of Sarena's mouth. "I hate them."

"Then defy them. Be glad they didn't take Lila. I don't know if her sweet soul could have endured it."

Again, the rusted echo tumbled through Sarena's lips. "I hate them."

"You need more than hate now, Sarena. Without your mind, the curse will take you. Iryatha has no mercy for those who enter her realm of darkness and pain."

"She's a myth."

"Then shed some light on this world. Show the people that they don't need to fear this curse."

Before agreeing, Sarena gazed on the funeral pyre of her order. The brilliant taste of fire refused to stop roaring, offering only ever-blinding light.

***

When the branches overhead parted, Sarena thought she'd gone blind. After squinting, the light washed over her.

Her vision adjusted. Azure curtains of sky hung overhead, while small trickles of blood drained downward. The witch sloshed through the last stretches of the swamp, shifting back and forth to dodge the crimson skin floating closer.

A fizzing sound made her snap to the left. Armie let go of her, leaving her to splash face first into the water.

For a moment, she saw the greenish-brown universe surrounding her limbs and body. A tiny fish swam by, pedaling moth wings from its sides. Sarena tasted vomit and forced herself up.

The priest cradled his left hand. His lips anchored downward in a frown. "It stings." A blister rose from one of his fingers, leaving his fingernail intact as the tip widened.

"No time to linger," Joseph said from ahead. He flashed his sword downward once again, still without penetrating the surface of the water.

Where had that fish gone? It was not a breed Sarena had ever seen.

The witch took in several deep breaths. Her chest hurt when she tried to speak, more so after tasting the swamp itself. "Keep… Go…" She spat to the side.

Her saliva struck a crimson patch, making it bubble like goosebumps.

Armie screamed. He lifted his left hand, covered in a thousand shaking blisters. Each grew a darker shade of red, though a tiny dot swam about within each one.

"Keep your voice down, man. Anything could be out here."

"Skin." Sarena wrapped her left arm around the priest. She pulled on him even as her own strength threatened to exhaust. "Toxic."

"Really?" The Legionnaire's arms sank as he rolled his eyes. "Must I always be the dashing hero?"

Current rippled against Sarena's chest. She looked down. The silhouette of a butterfly faded into the murky waters.

"It's." She pulled, trying to block out the constant string of screams. The priest's legs went limp. Her own eyes became too heavy to keep open.

In her mind, the defiler emissary approached, his manic tongue lapping with hunger.

Sarena forced her eyes open. "No." She lifted her trembling fingers toward Joseph. "No."

The dark-shaded fighter stopped. Water sloshed around him. "Make up your mind. Don't be a hero if you're about to die."

Shaking her head, the witch lifted her staff from the swamp. Mud gripped on the shaft, refusing to let go. A drip of deep green ran over Sarena's fingers, making her hands tremble even more.

Ripples of water darted out around her. Her limbs shook, but she felt cold scales slither past as well.

She struck down with her staff. Bluish-white light swayed under her feet.

The missing phrase burrowed in her mind.

Armie howled louder. His voice hadn't weakened from the strain. When his blistered hand sank into the swamp, his voice shrieked louder.

"This will do us no good if you both die before you can get out of the swamp."

"Shut." The witch pulled the priest onward, watching at the dots within his blisters grew. "Up."

"It's so pleasant to hear a complete sentence pass your lovely lips once more. Perhaps you could divine a way to get out of the water now."

The priest continued to scream.

"Or perhaps cast a spell to force your friend to be silent. Either will do."

Sarena's teeth locked together. The muck under her feet still glowed enough to show her the swamp had grown empty, save for the constant swell of mud.

A line of fire cut into her elbow. The grip on her staff almost fell loose.

She pushed her arm forward, drawing it away from the edge of a crimson band.

"They're getting closer," Joseph said. "I'm not sure what you're trying to prove, but you need to hurry."

Sarena would have said she was trying, but half a word would have cost too much breath.

"Perhaps if you let go of the priest."

"No."

For an instant, she stood on the icy field, the last time she remembered the complete phrase. The pieces linked together in her mind.

A dozen crystal orbs filled the air over the crown of Sarena's head. The lowest two sizzled against the surface of the water for a moment before blinking out.

The witch tasted her rage, the vomitous flavor of the swamp, the lingering salt of Night's Edge in her mouth.

Under the waves, her fingers snapped around Armie's arm. Above the water, her grip locked onto the staff. The witch marched forward. She knew this moment was death, but she stomped onward.

At the moment of her death, just before the curse tasted her flesh, she'd seen a Legionnaire dash at her. Sarena drew back her staff, filling her limbs with power.

"I would hope you aren't planning on killing me," Joseph said.

Sarena blinked. She was still in the swamp, not on a frozen field surrounded by an army of fiends driven mad by the emptiness in their souls.

You need more than hate now, Elissa said. So long gone, but her friend still spoke to her.

"Pouch." The witch pulled the priest forward. The mohawked man's mouth still wavered in agony, but his voice trailed off.

"Bottle." She pulled deep on her diaphragm and lungs. "Blue... herbs. Bright. Green. Leaf."

"Oh damn. You're trying to give me a bloody recipe."

Bobbing in the sludge, the witch nodded as best she could. "Heat.

Broth. Blisters."

"Do you have enough for his entire hand?"

"Arm. Yes."

Looking both ways, she found the patches of red swaying back toward her. They might have searched for her or been flowing back to their original places. Maybe they grew from the constant overflow from the wall around Siken. Contact meant more blisters, all burning and nurturing tiny ampules within her flesh.

Dragging the priest closer, Sarena held Armie close. Murky sludge swayed against them, but it was better than the stinging skin discarded from the wall above.

The witch looked forward, feeling the faintness of her skin, the shortness of her breath. Her elbow felt as though it lingered over the top of cook pot.

She slumped to the side, making sure she drifted at the Legionnaire.

The water and the weight took her.

***

A silver gown of scales and flesh hung in the darkness. Mucus dripped from the hem, forming a subtle pool along the stone floor.

Sarena could see her breath. In the distance, an empty purple haze lit the deep chamber.

"You have found my wedding dress."

The witch turned, whipping her head back and forth in search of the shallow voice. "Who are you?"

"Their Queen. I am embedded within each of them."

"Each of who? The defilers?"

"If that is what you wish to call them." The Queen shifted at the edge of the shadows, her body swaying as much as it slithered, flowing as much as it floated.

"You aren't human."

"I heal the gaps."

Sarena turned around, unable to find her staff. The spell to generate light drifted out of her thoughts.

"You aren't close enough to comprehend me."

"Are you a dweller?" the witch asked.

The Queen stopped. Her many-curved silhouette stopped pacing through the chamber. "I have heard that term. It is how witches speak of my birth mothers." A head shifted close to the violet light, enough to reveal streaming, swirling locks. "Yes. I was a dweller."

"But no longer."

"No longer. I am Queen. I am the mother of guidance. A thousand of my children gestate within your arm. Ten thousand mature within the priest's hand."

"What do you want with the people of Siken?"

"You aren't close enough to comprehend."

The witch breathed deep. The air frosted her lungs. "How can I get closer?"

"Enter my city. I will show you the way."

***

She woke, puking water and mud over her immodest chest.

Warm air drifted around Sarena. She looked at the line on her arm. A bruised line crept around her elbow, but no blisters remained.

Something boiled a few feet away. Steam rose from a small kettle sitting between Sarena and Joseph. Armie lay on his side, his hand enveloped in bandages.

Joseph's eyes lit up when he saw the witch was awake. "Our Sun Maiden rises with her master's zenith."

She looked up. The largest of the suns hovered overhead.

"How long was I out?" Her hoarse voice didn't scratch at her neck, though it still creaked with exhaustion.

"Two hours. Maybe three."

She nodded at the priest. "How is he?"

"I don't know. The salve you mentioned worked so fast you both stopped mumbling."

"Mumbling?"

Joseph nodded. "Yes. He kept saying something about how she could see him. You kept saying 'the queen.' It was all quite distracting."

"Did anything come out of the swamp?"

"No, but we won't be going back."

Sarena glanced down the arid slope. The bands of crimson skin had congealed and widened, stretching through the path they'd come.

"We'll get into the city," the Legionnaire said. "It might be wise if you rest for a while. The priest has yet to show any sign of waking up himself."

The witch knew she needed to rest, but the sins kept drifting on. When night fell, the defilers would storm out of Siken again—unless they had a reason to stay in the city.

***

Under the blanket of the Skyborn Range, they ran. Three witches, smiling and laughing because the youngest of their group had suggested doing something foolish.

Lila ran several paces ahead of Elissa and Sarena. All three left bootprints in the moist late winter grass.

"I hope you two are aren't letting me outrun you."

Elissa laughed. "What if I am?" She had the most to carry between her wide-brimmed hat, staff, and bardiche.

"Then catch up." Lila's pace quickened. Bits of mud lifted into the air behind her steps.

Sarena shook her head.

Elissa poked Sarena with the base of her staff. "Don't be so sour about it."

"Huh?"

The blonde witch shifted the head of her staff in a circle. A faint aura surrounded her hips and feet. Within a few seconds, Elissa trotted closer to Lila.

"About time one of you caught up to me." The light bounce of Lila's voice made Sarena smile, even from so far away. "Hey, turtle-feet! What's keeping you back there?"

Just as quickly, the smile faded from Sarena's face. As slim as she might be, she had no spell to increase her speed, nor endurance to help her push closer.

Sarena had read from the Book of Nexial Bindings. The most diluted of bindings passed her lips in a whisper. She stared at the boots and ankles of the other witches while they ran. Bright teal coils reached out of the open air, snagging the legs of the other witches. Lila stumbled forward, smashing an imprint into the ground. Elissa tripped, landing on her hands and knees.

Trotting past, Sarena gave a slight wave to each. "I thought this was a race. Why are you two taking a break?"

Muddied scowls were the only answer either woman gave. The witch laughed as she ran along.

She only released the bindings after she was a long distance ahead.

***

It would something other than brute force to stop the defilers. They had greater physical strength and stamina, just as they had the capability to grow faster and stronger still.

Sarena thought about that last race, the first race she ran with both of her sisters in arms. What would they have thought about Siken? Would Elissa agree to burn the city? Would Lila have fled to protect the villagers first-hand?

Armie sat up, massaging his bandaged knuckles. "What hit me?"

The witch continued to lay on the slope. Joseph lay uphill, cradling Night's Edge like a child holding his favorite toy. Below, the swamp continued to congeal with more of the crimson skin.

"I think the defilers have twisted the swamp to their own purpose. The wall isn't their outer boundary, at least it won't be for much longer."

The priest held up his hand. "This is why the wall bleeds. It wraps a scab over the land and water." He glanced up and his face drooped. "They even threaten the sky."

Clouds of grayish-brown drifted from the city. The drab stain lightly erased the clear sky.

"If we go, we shall breathe their smoke long before setting our own fires."

Armie tilted his head. "Do you still want to go?"

"I never wanted to go. I wanted enough coins to get into the Sanctum." Sarena's spine itched, especially the circular scar on her back. She whispered when she spoke again. "I don't know if anyone can take this mark away from me."

The witch pulled out her roll, unfastening its latches. Her dress, the constant defense around her body, had taken so many cuts and tears, it threatened to degrade into ribbons along the lowest edges. The bodice, waist, and most of the skirt remained unblemished, aside from several scattered nicks.

Whispering, the priest said, "May the Sky Lord see fit to protect your soul. May his light offer you peace."

"Save your prayers for those who truly need them." Sarena flared out the length of her dress before drawing the black cloth over her head.

"If I cannot give prayers for our defender, then who will ever be worthy?"

Sarena didn't bother answering.

***

The suns drifted lower still, the first prepared to embrace an unseen sky.

Joseph woke and drew a cloth from his pocket. Without a greeting, he wiped the onyx surface of Night's Edge.

Still massaging his bandaged hand, Armie asked, "How did you rest, good sir?"

"Not half as comfortably as I'd have liked. The bed was far too lumpy and lacked a damsel on either of my sides." The Legionnaire shifted his watch and smiled. "Certainly no Sun Maiden to warm my heart either."

Warmth filled Sarena's cheeks as she shifted away. She'd set to cleaning her staff so it wouldn't be mired with any remnants of the swamp.

Armie checked the position of his knives and straightened his robe. "Then we're ready to go on?"

The Legionnaire rose, swaying his weapon through a few basic positions. "That entirely depends on you as the most wounded member of our company."

The priest drew in a deep breath, then gave a single nod. "I think I can manage."

"We venture into likely death. Not a problem for myself or the lovely Maiden, but a mortal might find impalement a troubling ailment to overcome."

"Impalement?"

"Or disembowelment. You premature demise in most cases, if not my own as well. Do you think you can manage or will you soon be visited by any degree of certainty?"

Sarena finished wiping at the base of her staff. "I think you've tormented him quite enough."

"Better I torment him than the defilers of Siken. Just what rest do you think we'll find once we get in there?"

"None." The witch stood and walked away from the last of the swamp canopy. She looked up at the wall, seeing the tall lines, dividing it into segments.

Blood failed to follow the structured canals, rumbling from one section to the next on a long descent. "You're going to cost me two more coins before this is over."

She positioned her feet on the bottom edge of the steep ascent. If they climbed, the would soon be at the true base of the wall.

"You don't mean to build a fountain, do you?"

Armie glanced back and forth. "What sort of fountain?"

"My order discovered that unliving are bound to localized points. When we die, our bodies rematerialize at those points when we're restored."

"She either builds a fountain or we revive back in our pits. Assuming, of course, that we'll die when we enter the city."

Looking up the slope, Sarena said, "We have to get to the base of the wall next. We're not inside yet."

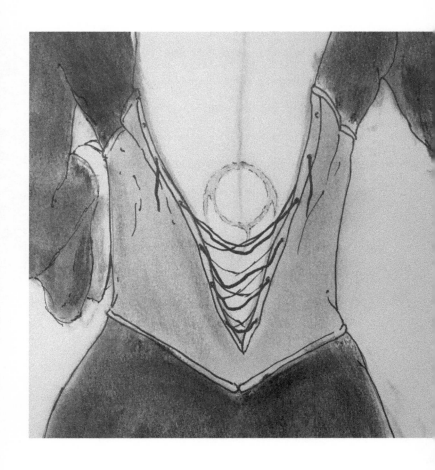

SINS OF THE PAST

A channel of dirt burst under Sarena's foot. The slope turned from solid ground to dust in less than an instant. The witch thrust the base of her staff into the ground, bracing herself against the crumbling surface.

Overhead, the wall of Siken still loomed and still bled.

"I must say, this is not the most stable climb I could have imagined." Joseph had continued his flippant mutterings as he climbed the dry slope. He'd already complained about a thicket scratching the palm of his hand, as well as his desire to find a more secure route upward.

None of them wished to step near the blood flowing down from the towering wall.

Rather than offer a response to the Legionnaire, Sarena looked to her left. Armie fought his way upward, despite the layers of wrap limiting his ability to grab onto the slope. "We're almost there," the witch said.

The priest smiled for an instant, before using his elbow to brace his next step.

Under her hands, the faint strands of brown grass strained to reach deep enough into the soil. Inside Sarena's grasp, their roots loosened and they tumbled. A few blades of grass dangled from the slope while others fell toward the crimson embrace of the swamp.

Grabbing another clump of dirt, Sarena felt the sting of dehydration in her fingers. She saw a strained hand with skin so dried it had become a sheet of worn leather draped over thin bones.

Joseph punched the slope three times. "No. I am whole." He clenched his teeth and eyes. "I will remain."

"Keep climbing, Legionnaire."

The man winced, turning his head away from the witch.

"I said keep climbing."

He snapped a hand upward.

Though her arms blazed, Sarena forced herself to do the same. Her hands withered to scraps of skin and bone. She locked her eyes shut, praying the moment might pass.

In the dark, a dweller's tentacles swept out, reaching for her. Beyond, a feminine shape hovered within a floating cask—

A hand on her shoulder called her back. The witch opened her eyes. Armie rested on the steep incline, bracing himself as he touched Sarena's shoulder.

"Come back," he said. "We're almost there."

Joseph hoisted himself over the top ridge. The same point lay only a few grasps outside of Sarena's reach.

Burrowing the bottom of her staff into the ground, the witch pushed herself upward. Armie continued his pace, climbing with his elbows and knees when his hand reached its limit.

***

On top of the ridge, the trio stopped, all three breathing deep.

The Legionnaire sat on the edge, leaving his legs on the steep incline. Armie knelt looking down.

Sarena sat at the top of the slope, as close as she could be to the wall without touching it. With no wind, she looked back across the valley. A ring of huts and tents lay beyond the swamp. Dots fumbled in the distance, villagers straggling behind.

The witch closed her eyes, mourning the added pain and suffering those few would endure. Every verbal jab they hurled at her lingered in her frown.

"Is that the village?" Joseph asked.

Sarena nodded.

"Will the stragglers have time to escape?"

"Maybe." The witch glanced at Armie. She knew her true feelings could crush his spirit faster than anything in Siken.

Joseph stood. "Then it may best be time for us to push our own attack. Priest, how do we push into the city?"

Armie looked up. "I need a moment."

"No time. While we wait, the rest of your people die. Already…" The Legionnaire lifted his index finger, tallying the stragglers from far away. "Seven linger near their campfires. Can they hold off the normal assault of these defilers? What about any escalation we might cause?"

"There's no reason to say that."

"The generosity of a Sun Maiden's words. Will it provide a proper salve once we've angered the defilers within?"

"We didn't have as smooth of a trek through the swamp as you did."

Joseph drew the sword from his back. "Night's Edge has specific tastes. And specific hungers."

Sarena stood, making sure every strain in her joints was visible. Her hand rose in a gesture of peace. "I am grateful for your help before."

The Legionnaire bobbed his head. "It is my honor to serve one who is deserving. Now, priest—"

The witch wrapped her fingers around Joseph's throat, swinging to the side. She pinned Joseph against the wall. "For one moment, I would appreciate you holding your tongue."

"You seek a kiss." The Legionnaire smiled. "It might be mine, though Night's Edge may wish to kiss you first."

Sarena gritted her teeth and leaned toward Joseph's face. "I've had one kiss from Night's Edge already."

Joseph's brow rose.

"Surprised? So was I." The fragments of memory wandered around Sarena's mind. Segments sometimes bumped into each other, but rarely stayed in place for long. "When we first met, you were almost lost. The Legion of Flame had long since fallen."

From behind the witch, Armie rose. "What?"

"All of you swam in the abyss of madness. No thought. No desire. Someone drove you toward every stronghold capable of standing up to the dwellers. One by one, you slaughtered every person on hand."

Joseph's mouth fell open.

"Killing wasn't enough for your mistress."

***

Before Sarena saw the bodies, she smelled bile and blood. A roar of voices and armor clashes stopped her when she stepped outside the front gate.

Elissa launched onto the snowy field of the Keep, its curved blade of her polearm blocked the most enraged fighters at the front of the pack. With a single twist, the blonde witch pushed aside incoming blades and hacked into her attackers' limbs.

The onyx-bladed Legionnaire locked onto Elissa and charged into the air. A gravelly hiss erupted from his split lips. Empty eyes glared at the blonde with hunger and hate.

Elissa thrust her bardiche upward, pushing through the Legionnaire's half-decayed chest. Globs of ichor chugged out of the wound. The same fluid drooled out of the Legionnaire's mouth.

Still, he hungered. With one hand, he swept the onyx sword at Elissa.

The blonde witch shifted her head back from the first attack. When the second sweep came, she jumped back, leaving her weapon in the wild commander's side.

He dropped to one knee, locking eyes with Elissa before rising again. The long polearm dangled from the Legionnaire's side, forcing him to flail with each step. Slashing the air in front of him, the Legionnaire's march steadied once more.

Elissa shifted to a defensive stance, shifting her staff in an arc. A crisp azure radiance warped into a bubble around the blonde witch.

The Legionnaire darted forward. The bardiche flapped at his side, ignored in a flash of steady speed.

A barrage of slashes sparked the ethereal barrier, tossing blue and black glitter into the air.

Elissa thrust forward with the head of her staff. The impact would have winded a larger man. The Legionnaire ignored it and hissed again. A spray of ichor speckled Elissa's face.

The blonde witch thrust with her staff again, then dove left. Her hand grasped the base of her bardiche. Screaming, she started steering the Legionnaire to the ground.

Sarena lifted her own staff, gathering her strength. Phrases scattered and converged in her mind, though they all shared a single target. Her feet launched forward, kicking up snow as she charged.

With two weapons extending the reach of her arms, Elissa pushed the Legionnaire down to one knee. He slashed at the blonde witch, barking and hissing with each stroke. Elissa lifted or lowered her weapons, keeping away from the Legionnaire's attacks.

Feeling the phrases congeal, Sarena cast a binding around the man's arms so Elissa could finish him. She felt the loops form around the Legionnaire's wrists. Jabbing the base of her staff into the man's back, the witch pulled his arms to the ground, ready to be locked in place.

A ball of darkness and fire exploded between Elissa and the Legionnaire, knocking both witches to the ground. Dark flames subsided. Trails of smoke revealed a female figure with a filigreed mask. Shadows and sparks erupted from the woman's hand as she punched Elissa in the chest. A plume of light burst from behind the blonde witch.

Sarena reached out with her left hand. "No!" A foot smashed down on her neck.

Overhead, the Legionnaire gazed down at the witch, shifting the onyx sword in a flourish. With the tip aimed down, he thrust the blade into Sarena's mouth. She tasted metal and blood.

***

Joseph's lungs bellowed out in agony. Sarena felt the same stinging in the fingers she still kept around the Legionnaire's throat.

The silvery-brown surface behind Joseph shifted. Its segments folded outward, pushing against his shoulders and torso.

Snapping her free hand around one of Joseph's arms, the witch started to pull. The Wall of Siken bit into her knuckles.

Through her screaming, the witch saw Armie rush to the Legionnaire's side. Veins popped up near the priest's blue mohawk. He leaned back, dragging the Legionnaire away from the Wall.

All three landed on the top of the slope. A stream of crimson flowed from the Wall, washing past Sarena and down the slope before enveloping the edge of the swamp.

Dozens of little cuts bled on Joseph's back. Two more marks drew blood from Sarena's knuckles.

On the Wall itself, needle-thin lines of blood drained into the surface. The barbs retracted, leaving a glossy finish to the towering barrier.

A dingy brown colored most of the Wall, though embedded towers grew darker between each section. Blood drew out even the finest seams within the Wall. The constant rush of crimson painted wide stains over the top, draining toward the earth. Above the swamp, more trails of crimson incubated creatures Sarena had yet to fathom.

The witch looked at her hand. No blisters lifted from the cuts.

Joseph tried to stand, but the witch snapped a hand on his shoulder. "Wait."

She pulled back the collar of his jacket. Dozens of cuts dotted his shoulder blades, but none bubbled with blisters.

"You don't have enough to treat my entire back."

"No, but I don't need to." Sarena let go of the Legionnaire and stepped a few steps away from him. "It's a bunch of little cuts, nothing unusual about them."

Armie released a loud exhale. "How fortunate."

Joseph stood up. "Indeed. A pity that the swamp wasn't as benign."

The priest pointed down. "It's growing."

Sarena nodded. "There are smaller pools outside of the swamp. Whatever is inside Siken, it's leaking."

"Wonderful," Joseph said. "And entire city of aggressive blood waiting to kill us all."

The witch extended her wounded hand, holding it close to the Wall's surface. The silvery glaze dried. Dozens of barbs poked out, unable to reach Sarena's skin. "It knows we're here."

Armie drew one of his curved knives. "Who knows?"

"Someone in the city. Or something." Sarena shook her head. "The Wall knows we're here too."

The surface shifted, extending and retracting barbs near Sarena's hand. None could get close enough.

Armie howled and thrust his knife into the shifting surface. Only the tip pierced the Wall's outer membrane. Mucus dripped down the edge of the blade, dropping off before it could touch the priest's arm. "There is a life to this thing. It hungers like any beast." He pulled the knife away, wiping it on the sleeve of his robe. "The only toll it will accept is food."

Joseph touched the base of Night's Edge to the palm of his hand. "If it is so desperate for blood, then it can taste mine." His hand locked around the weapon, grinding upward toward the sword's tip. Maroon stains smudged the onyx metal.

The witch turned toward the Legionnaire, her hands extended. "You don't know that it wants blood. It could be an emotional trigger."

"Then we should learn what it wants."

Joseph lifted Night's Edge over his head and slashed downward. The sword scraped the surface, screeching like it had struck a metal shield. Shimmering mucus drained onto the naked ground while barbs flaked from the

Wall. A darker layer emerged, squirming like a small animal trying to escape after being swallowed whole.

The Legionnaire flashed his weapon downward, flinging off the excess blood and mucus. "Perhaps now would be a good time to set aside our differences?"

"Perhaps." Sarena approached the wriggling layer, watching the subtle shifts under its moist skin. She shook her head. "I never imagined the Wall would actually be alive."

Several slithers moved to the surface, curling in arcs until they made a ring. Three prongs burst from the surface, each releasing a trickle of glossy fluid.

All three travelers lifted their closest weapons.

After the stream drained from each prong, the sharp points curled downward, stabbing back into the Wall. Two hooked in at the sides of the ring, the third descended from a point close to the bottom.

Sarena and Joseph lowered their weapons. The priest looked at his companions and the stagnant design. "I don't understand."

"You couldn't," the Legionnaire said. He kicked a cloud of dust down the slope.

"I'm surprised you didn't recognize it." Sarena loosened the laces of her dress. She turned, letting the low-cut back slip close to her bottom. "Every unliving body has a mark in their flesh. Not just a scar, but the same scar." The witch tapped a finger against her lower back, feeling the same symbol that had emerged from the Wall.

Armie crouched, examining the witch's mark. "It's the same." He looked up. "Is it the same on him?"

"I haven't looked at it." Sarena shifted her dress back in place and tightened the laces. "I have seen others. Those who lose themselves to the curse are nothing more than a rotten body animated by that mark. It is only an emblem, but it's usually close to where we were struck…"

She thought of the woman in the filigreed mask. The hand burning with shadows.

The priest stood. "I have an idea." He rolled up his sleeve, extending his bandaged hand.

"Don't be a fool—"

Armie pressed his hand against the curse mark on the Wall. The barrier's skin quaked for a moment, then became still. "It didn't react to me." He stepped away. "I think it will react to the two of you, though I do not know how much."

To the side, Joseph examined his sword. "It may try to kill us."

"With everything we've seen the defilers do, they could easily reach further than a hand's width. Yet this wall does nothing more than extend barbs from its surface."

Sarena knew the priest had an idea but hadn't expressed it. "You have a deeper theory."

"I do. The outer layer is a defense and feeding mechanism. The true wall, the one showing the curse mark, has not shown hostility or a defense mechanism."

From behind, Joseph said, "It's waiting for one of us."

"Yes." Armie nodded at the Legionnaire. "That's it exactly."

"What would you have us do?" Sarena asked.

"Touch the wall. Briefly, to ensure its intent. If it reacts, we can adjust accordingly."

The Legionnaire moved close to the others again. "And if it does nothing?"

"We find another way. I haven't seen any gates along this wall, not even one a defiler could use."

Sarena pulled up her left sleeve. "He has a point." She walked toward the exposed layer, holding out her hand.

"And you mean to just do as the priest says?"

"It makes sense, and it's only for a moment."

"You pushed me against that same wall for a moment." Joseph leaned toward the witch's ear. "I can still feel the scratches."

"This time, it's not your hand touching the wall."

He stepped back and crossed his arms. "Don't expect me to save you."

Sarena draped her fingers onto the clammy skin above the scar emblem. The sensation was much like touching another person, but the surface was much colder. "Nothing so far."

She kept shifting her gaze over the exposed wall, wondering what sort of barb might shoot out. Where could a crab squeeze out? Far above, nodules opened in scattered field of glands where none were close to the others.

The witch pressed her palm against the curse emblem. Her bosom rose higher with each breath. The Wall's pulse raced faster, still refusing to move in any way. "You're in there," she whispered. "You know we're here and you haven't sent us away. Open a door so we might talk."

Within the Wall, a shadow stirred. Flopping forms lurched forward, pressing against the surface skin. The outline of a hand, a foot, a shoulder, all appeared, assembled in the wrong order. Too many limbs, too few eyes. The faces gazed out, wailing without sound inside the fleshy membrane. Veins pumped blood through the skin. A few tributaries branched into the bodies swirling within the towering barricade.

Higher and higher, the shapes flailed. A hundred palms pushed against the wall. A thousand toes kicking under the impossible skin. The myriad extended in every direction, shaking the wall within each segment.

Arms and legs reached out. Heads strained to stay bound to their necks as their faces gasped for the surface. All stayed wrapped in a layer of skin.

But it was a layer that stretched.

Armie whimpered and slumped to his knees. He curled his hands behind his head and rocked back and forth. "Lotac save us. Lotac save us. Lotac save us." The priest mumbled the same words, cycling them with the trembling of his body.

Sarena grabbed his shoulder and shook him. "Armie? What is it? What's wrong?"

"Lotac save us. Lotac save us."

The Legionnaire pulled Armie up with one hand. "Dammit man, snap out of it." He backhanded the priest. "What is it with you?"

Sarena jerked Armie around and slapped his face once. "What's wrong? Say something."

The priest's lower lip quaked enough for a pearl of drool to rappel off his chin. With one finger, he pointed to the wall. "Hamner..." Armie looked away from the wall.

On the surface, a face stretched out of the membrane. The buzz of a priest's mohawk traced a line on the center of the writhing head.

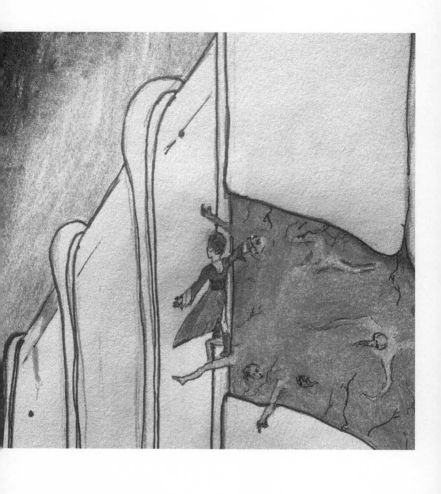

THE WALL

Armie whimpered and cried as his face dangled over the slope leading down from the Bleeding Wall.

Faces and contorted limbs continued to push against the membrane holding the wall together. Veins pumped defiled sludge through the massive barrier.

Still set in the center of the open layer, the curse mark shifted upward toward a mass of anguished limbs.

Sarena looked along the line where the mark passed, then shook her head. Body parts pressed out on a steady incline. The top and bottom of the line were marked by a dense extension of curled fingers and angry kicks. A few screaming faces pressed through the gaps.

It all remained steady, protruding.

Intact.

"We climb," the witch said.

"Climb what?" Joseph bit his lower lip. "You act as if there is a ladder
—"

"Stairs. Sort of." Sarena grabbed a wrist and an ankle hovering over her head. "We use what we must. Make sure he goes next, then follow." The witch pressed her left toe on the back of a neck. "Don't fall behind."

As she lifted herself up, the witch saw the path ahead protrude further. Limbs extended all the way to the shoulder or groin, never revealing anything beyond—especially not a wound.

"Up you go," Joseph said. "No need to be shy."

Still, the priest mumbled. "Hamner. Lotac save me."

"Yes, yes, Lotac save you. I'm sure you'll have a better view of the sky from the top."

Sarena reached upward. The only hold in reach was a woman's scowling face. The witch slapped her hand on the wall. Under the surface skin, the woman shook her head. A chill raced deep into Sarena's palm.

"Dammit, man. Move. Weep while you climb."

Below, the priest shook his head. "No. No."

Sarena's brow grew heavy. "Armie, keep climbing."

He shook his head.

Joseph shrugged. "I don't see how this is going to work. He keeps whimpering like a baby."

"My brother…"

Tension locked the witch's jaw. "Iriyatha's own luck." She shook her head. "Armie. Armie! It is getting dark and your friends are counting on you. Now you can cry or you can get your holy ass up here and do something to help."

The priest glared up. "That's my brother—"

"Then get up here and do something about it. Help him."

Below, the mohawked head shifted. Behind the glaze of skin, it glared at the priest. Even from above the others, Sarena could see the scowl on Hamner's face.

"You'd best do it," the Legionnaire said. "I still have business to attend with the Sun Maiden."

The priest grabbed an arm and stepped on a foot.

Quietly, Sarena sighed before she returned to her own climb. In front of her, a head emerged, the only non-human face.

The emissary's tongue wagged within the wall's skin, his eyeless face pushed forward. The ridges in the emissary's head stretched the wall to its limit.

She climbed.

The emissary shifted back into the wall.

Sarena reached for an arm with a closed fist. The hand turned, bearing its wrist for the witch. When her fingers closed around the limb, the hand opened. Inside, the emissary's diamond-shaped mouth stuck out. His wet tongue licked the witch's pinky finger.

Her hand snapped back.

Joseph called out. "What is it?"

"The…" She shook her head. The tongue kept lapping in her direction. "Someone's trying to scare us."

"Then it's wise that you left me to guard the rear. I would have left the frightened children behind."

Sarena grabbed the wrist and jerked it away from the wall. The limb locked, extended within the wrapper of skin. With her opposite hand, the witch struck the wall's elbow. A tiny snap bubbled underneath.

Every limb shifted under the witch's feet.

She scrambled to steady herself, climbing through a pasture of frantic limbs and angry faces. The emissary pushed his face through, watching her, judging her.

Sarena grabbed his tongue and stretched herself to reach the next row of ankles and chests.

"What…" A grumble curled from below the witch and the priest. "How did you piss off a wall that was willing to let you climb it?"

A fleshy defiler-coated priest climbs halfway out of the wall. He punched Sarena, knocking her back. The neuter body flailed its arms, enveloped in wall skin instead of robes.

Hamner struck Sarena's face twice. She scowled, thrusting her palm under his jaw. With an overhead swing, she smashed down at the fleshy priest. Purple ooze curdled from Hamner's eyes and nose.

"You wanted us here." Sarena's eyes narrowed, looking for any sign of the emissary.

The defiler's wagging tongue drifted within the same hand looming beside the witch's waist.

She grabbed the muscle, driving her nails in to the best of her ability. "If you wanted to torment us, you could have done it anywhere. If you want us in Siken, why hinder us?"

Each finger pushed against the witch's hand. That level of force hadn't struck her since she was pelted with rocks by a caravan of pilgrims. She let go.

Pushing up from Hamner's back, the emissary's head emerged, this time without his trademark tongue. His diamond-shaped mouth vibrated against the flap of skin binding him to the wall. "We seek your worth. She calls for those who are marked. She wants to know your hatred."

"What hatred? I'm trying to protect innocent people."

"She wishes to protect the innocent. She would know why you fight her and claim her goals."

Joseph spoke from below. "She? Who is this?"

"She says you do not understand." The emissary tilted his head. "No. She says I do not understand. I must allow you to climb and see what she feels." The defiler spokesman merged back into Hamner's back. The fleshy priest retracted into the wall, leaving purple stains where he'd burst forth.

Sarena shook her head. "We can debate it later. Climb."

***

At the last handhold, the witch grabbed a thick ridge of bone, pulling herself on top of the wall. A crimson smear coated her arms and legs, but she felt no wounds. Looking down at the bone ridge, a stream of blood as wide as her hand trailed downward.

Dark gray smoke lifted from beyond the wall. White steam flushed at Sarena in bursts.

She knelt at the edge, extending a more reliable hand for Armie and Joseph. When the priest rose to the top of the wall, his eyes stared at some invisible point, his pupils widened more than necessary for a sunlit day.

When the witch reached down for Joseph, he shook his head. "I've had my share of risks on this particular ascent, thank you." He pulled himself up using the same bone ridge.

"I still need your help to get through this."

"I have no doubt of that." The Legionnaire glanced at a drop of the wall's blood on his hand. After flicking the drop away, he said, "There's no way I can know how much you crave revenge."

"You killed me."

"If I hadn't, someone else would have. At least my way, you're still in our esteemed company."

"You're not going to try to excuse yourself?"

He shrugged. "Why should I? You'll judge me as much as the people of Siken."

The witch shook her head. "That's not fair."

"Isn't it?" Joseph stepped away, looking over the smoke-filled sky.

Sarena rubbed the inside corner of her right eye. A dull throb rushed behind her eyes.

Armie's voice had shattered, falling deeper into a low tone. "Where do we go from here?"

"I'm not sure."

Joseph kicked the hide-colored surface with the heel of his foot. "There's nothing to see and nowhere to go."

"There's a way." The witch dug in her satchel, lifting her coin purse. She drew two of her golden emblems just as her eyelids took on a tremor. "Each coin carries with it an innate power. Ten open a gateway to the Sanctum."

"I somehow doubt you have ten."

Closing her teeth together, she ignored the Legionnaire's statement. "One can restore flesh or call on stronger spells for an instant." Rubbing the coins together in her hand, Sarena said, "Two can build an Anchor."

Joseph smiled. Cackling, he slapped his knee. "Please. You're going to make an Anchor in this wall?" He howled with laughter again.

The witch took a coin in each hand and slapped them together. A burst of lightning shot between her joined fingers. Light flared as she pulled the coins apart. Between her hands, a coiled length of metal gleamed like a mirror in sunlight. The handle in her right hand sparked with flames, reminding Sarena of the woman who scarred her back.

Screaming, the witch shared the words to seal the power between her hands. "Instill the fire!" She swept to one knee and thrust the end of the iron into the wall. Bursting like lava, light fumed around the wound. The wall grew dark as charred sand, twisting into a font that filled with luminous water.

Sarena stepped back, allowing the fountain to dim enough to see. Water continuously poured into the elevated stone bowl, but it did not fall as rain or rise from a spring.

The witch cupped her hands, lifting the luminous water to her lips. When the liquid touched her lips, she glowed for a moment. The bloodstains washed away from her arms. Any bruises faded from her face.

"Joseph, drink."

The Legionnaire shook his head as his lips slipped open. "Indeed." He cupped his hands as Sarena had. When he drank, the same glow surrounded him, absolving his most recent wounds. "Truly, you are a Sun Maiden."

Armie dipped his hands into the fountain for an instant. Steam billowed from his wounded hand before he whipped his fingers back. "What happened?"

"You aren't cursed." Sarena closed her eyes and lowered her head. "It cannot heal you."

Joseph used one hand to take up more of the water. "The downside is that we restore here now."

"Better than a pit."

"Quite true." He drank again.

The priest looked at the dimmed section of wall beneath them, then looked to the sky. "Lotac, I thank you for the mighty weapon you have given us. I beseech you to bless us with another such strike."

Distantly, a voice called out to them. "You will find no such favor." The emissary stood atop the raised tower separating the section from the rest of the wall. "A witch may only buy so many favors."

Joseph spun, drawing Night's Edge from his back and dashing at the defiler.

The emissary slung one arm. A giant whip of bone and exposed muscle rose from the surface of the wall, slapping the Legionnaire away. The dark-skinned man groaned as he became a speck in the distance.

"Do not mistake a change in the surface as the death of this wall."

Sarena lifted her staff at a defensive angle and bumped her elbow against the priest's arm. "Draw your knives. You may not get another chance."

Armie lifted his blades with a soft song. Aiming the points at the emissary, both blades stayed parallel under Sarena's staff. The priest's bandaged hand kept a loose grip on one of the knives.

The emissary took a few slow steps forward. Beside him, the massive whip relaxed, though the tip swayed at its master's side.

Digging into her heart, the witch cast her inner strength into the staff. Luminous azure light flooded over the weapons, granting them greater strength.

"You have risen this high under your terms, but She will not let you go deeper. Not without sacrifice."

Sarena turned her staff, holding the power within. "You wanted us here. Or she did."

Another whip rose on the emissary's opposite side. "You will say it with reverence."

"Who is your mistress? What does she want with this city?"

"What does any creature want with the parts of its body? What opinion do you have of your fingers or your spleen?"

The priest shouted, spittle flew from his mouth. "What did you do to my brother?"

Turning toward Armie, the slits the emissary had instead of eyes fluttered and shut. "You may use a knife or a robe. She uses your brother."

"That doesn't mean anything."

From the corner of her eye, Sarena saw a ripple on the surface of her fountain. She needed time.

"I will show you Her wonder." The whips flared straight up and the emissary stood in just as rigid a pose. The gray smoke thinned, opening the shape of a second wall just beyond the first. Between the barriers, a dark red slush flowed close to the top. As it stilled, the vapors faded to nothing.

Beyond, the city's might endured on a foundation of spongy skin and mucus. Each building stood tall, a body of skeleton and bone latticed with an unspiderlike webbing. Bodies traversed the streets, marching at an even pace no matter their destination. Bogs of frothy pink bubbled in several open areas. A spire of sinew and secreted scales stood at the center of the city, making a shadow over the former town square.

Armie fell to his hands and knees. The knife in his bandaged hand clattered out of his grasp. "Lotac, god…" His head turned back and forth, slow with disbelief. "What is this?"

The ripple in the fountain grew faster.

"It is Her dream taking shape. Her strength grows as does her touch. Once She lingered in the catacombs of other worlds. Now? She rises and stretches out, her wonder joins with all things."

Armie stabbed one of his knives into the surface beneath him. Tightening his lips, he picked up the other knife. When he stood, he jerked the robe from his shoulders, letting it drift away in the wind. "Beast. Not even Iriyatha would corrupt the very land as you have."

"It is Her will."

Gleaming water overflowed from the fountain.

"I am a servant of Lotac, Prince of the Wind, son of the Sky Lord."

Gusts of air pushed around Armie. The fibers of his mohawk shook with the invisible current. "I am but one life, but I will strike at your heart. For the crime of this corruption, I will make you bleed."

A burst of fiery light erupted beside Sarena. She did not dodge it, instead taking a step toward the emissary.

Within the light, a shadow grew from burnt particles. Every bit of ash and soot rushed out from the distance, building a silhouette. The man, tall and muscular, stepped from the blinding orb. Joseph scowled, his face dried out, his eyes staring with beady intensity.

"Priest," he said, drawing Night's Edge. "The Legion of Flame kills dwellers."

The emissary shook his head. "She is no longer a dweller."

***

The Lady Marianna held Sarena's hand, leading the young girl into a domed chamber of onyx embossed with layers of gold. "Remain quiet," the lady said to the young girl. "Watch and remember."

Men and women knelt in block groups as the Emperor's Consuls entered from the far side of the chamber. Several knights with torches walked alongside, each wearing an emblem of fire made from quartz and gold. The First Consul entered last, wearing a cape marked by two of the fire emblems, both full of diamond luster instead of polished rock.

A dais loomed close to the curtains where Sarena watched with the

Lady Marianna. The elder woman discarded her wrinkles for the occasion and allowed her tresses to grow bright with a sunlit luster.

When the First Consul stood at the dais, he knelt for a moment, silently speaking to at least one of the gods.

The Lady Marianna bent over and said, "Stay here."

Sarena watched her teacher step into the light, showing off her crimson and gold robes. "For what purpose does the Emperor call upon the Sunlit Order?"

"Fair Lady." The First Consul drew a broadsword and held it in offering. "The Emperor pleads you bestow these men and women with your strength. Allow them to champion humanity and vanquish the dwellers who live beneath our lands."

"The gods do not care about these dwellers."

"Yet they seek our homes and our lives. Only light can harm them. And we have so little of it."

Lady Marianna raised her right hand. "Then a new order shall be made to create light where there is none. Such legions will be bound to this flame." Her hand ignited in a tongue of tortured fire before she pressed her palm into the sword. "Take this weapon and consecrate the brightest among you. Forge from them a true Legion of Flame."

***

Dragging his right leg behind him, the Legionnaire shambled toward the emissary. "I saw it in the darkness of unlife. A dweller rests in the heart of this city. She tried to call my name."

"Then you did not listen."

Sarena stepped between Armie and Joseph. "Can we take him?"

"Possibly, though the priest should stay back."

"I swore to draw his blood."

"Unfortunately, you didn't get cursed before coming up here."

"I still have one life to give."

The witch drew in a deep breath. "Don't waste it."

Extending his tendril-arms and wall whips, the emissary made an open gesture while approaching the others.

Sarena blasted at one of the whips, making it spasm wildly.

Joseph smiled and raced toward the opposite whip. The fleshy lash cracked against the surface of the wall, but the Legionnaire jumped over it. The momentum rolled him forward. He lunged with the inertia, piercing Night's Edge into the emissary's chest.

The defiler snapped both tendril arms around Joseph's neck. Flexing back his shoulders, the emissary tightened the Legionnaire's neck until it was no thicker than Sarena's staff—the same staff that thrashed the side of the emissary's face.

A single shift in the defiler's position tossed Joseph into the witch. Both collapsed back toward the fountain.

Joseph stared up with absolute stillness. Then he burst into a billion flakes of ash.

Sarena rushed forward, blazing her power into an ethereal blade bound to the head of her staff. Thrashing, she drew blood from emissary.

Once. Twice. Thrice.

A whip slammed onto her. The pressure cracked her pelvis in an instant. A bolt of lightning surged through her body, frying her eyes. Her fingers twitched, the staff tumbled out of her grasp. Within her chest, both of her lungs popped. Her lips puffed and puffed, trembling in the futility of lost air.

***

All black.

The night of nothing.

Sarena stood up, collapsing with the impossibility inside her chest. Her jaw drooped, but her palate could not shift to suck in the slightest puff of air.

Behind her, someone whispered her name.

She spun around, locking her fists tight. No one was there.

Still over her shoulder, the soft voice spoke again. "I see you everywhere."

The question sprang to her lips, but the witch could not speak. Her body could not process air, for there was none to breathe.

Thick tendrils swayed in the darkness, just out of view. Snow drifted to the ground them both. "Come to me. Lather yourself. Consume."

The witch opened her mouth. Fire burned the ring on her back.

At last, she screamed. Bile tumbled from her mouth, as did maggot-ridden clumps of her former lungs. She coughed and hacked. Only when she fell to her knees did the mass push upward.

Her over-dried mouth cracked as she growled. "No." Sarena snorted, gritted her teeth. "No."

All of her spells erupted, sending the tendriled figure swooping far into the darkness, deeper than any whisper. The witch took a deep breath, then another. Each burst of air in or out of her body forced her heart to pump faster.

Behind her eyes, the fragments drifted after the unseen speaker. Rage faded, leaving Sarena's body to shake.

In the dark, the witch remembered one spell. Hope forced her to smile in glee. She knelt, pushing her hand against the pool of unfathomable night. After one last breath, she flushed the power from her body and began to scry.

A DWELLER'S GIFT

As she stepped from the fountain, Sarena opened her hand. Blisters caked each knuckle. The skirt of her dress had torn all the way up her left leg. Her right sleeve was no longer a memory. Using will alone, she summoned the staff to her hand.

Bruises covered the sides of Armie's face. The bandages around his hand were brown and red. One of his knives lay broken at his feet.

Joseph's jacket had turned to rags and he tossed it aside. "Finally." His semi-aloof tone had faded.

The witch remembered the lost creature who first murdered her outside the Northern Keep.

The emissary swayed back and forth in a circle made by remains of seven whips. Blood crusted over the wall. "You came back." The defiler thrashed his arms downward. "You were to lather yourself and consume."

Wordlessly, Sarena snapped a bolt of blue from her staff. The light seared a hole in the emissary's chest.

After sucking in his tongue, a dark sludge poured from the defiler's diamond-shaped mouth.

Joseph howled. He ran at the emissary.

A tendril-arm shot out like a cannon. The impact sheared the Legionnaire's left arm from his shoulder.

"It is not you that She wants, but you have some worth."

Sarena smashed her staff against the emissary's face, knocking him away from Joseph. A muscular whip rose from the wall and smashed down—

The witch jumped back. In one swing, she drew an ethereal blade and severed the whip from its base.

As much as the whip wriggled, ash still erupted underneath it. Joseph was gone again.

"We can do it," Armie said. A deep scowl etched the priest's face. With a single nod, he added, "Together."

"No." The skin of Sarena's lower lip cracked as her mouth tightened. "You'll die."

"We're already dead. Some of you get to reclaim your lives afterward."

Another stream of bile burst from the emissary's mouth. The wounds in his chest began bubbling with the same thick secretion. He smoothed the paste with his tendril arms and slipped into a drunken stumble.

"Keep the whips off of me." Sarena thrust her staff down as she stood up straight. The fragmented phrases had fallen from her thoughts. All she dared focus on were the complete conjectures and the power they drew upon. Extending an ethereal blade from her staff, she rushed toward the emissary again.

Two whips rose ahead of her. Armie dashed forward, slashing into the left whip.

As the right whip fell, the witch side stepped and jumped forward. Her boots pushed against Armie's back before she launched over the stunned whip. Another whip burst from the wall, but Sarena slashed it. The end of the whip wriggled off the wall.

Resting on one knee, the emissary flared out his tendril-arms. "You cannot see. She has nearly solved it."

"I don't care." The witch swung down with her staff—

The emissary caught it. His sturdy skin crinkled and burst open close to the blue glow erupting from the head of Sarena's implement. "It is the one defense your order always had. It is about to go away."

Sarena pushed forward on the staff, but couldn't force it closer to the emissary. When the witch pulled back, the defiler wrapped a tendril around her weapon, forcing her toward his moist moist mouth.

"The light won't keep them away."

The witch jerked on her staff again, but failed under the defiler's growing strength. Sarena groaned as she felt the tendons in her wrist harden and tear.

"Dwellers," the emissary said. "Does that ease your rage?"

He let go of the staff, letting Sarena tumble backward.

***

"We have allowed these monstrosities to rise for too long," Lady Marianna said.

She led Sarena and Elissa to a cavernous chamber under the Shimmering Citadel. Unlike the gleaming stones outside of the Sky Lord's temple, this room was darkness, even darker than Ember Sanctuary where petitioners pleaded for aid. In this chamber, there were more torches, but less light. The fires burned wide and tall but cast only a flicker through the shadowy air.

At the center of the room, a brick well lingered. A smooth pool of oil rested at the top of the well.

"Why is this room so different?" Sarena asked.

Elissa jabbed her friend's shoulder. "Shh."

"Do not silence her," Lady Marianna said. "This is why you were brought here." She walked to the opposite side of the well. "After the Dark Princess betrayed the Sky Lord, holes began to open between the worlds. Even without crystals, beings from other realms chose to step into our world."

Holding her hand over the well, a purple and black tentacle snapped out of the oil. Lady Marianna stared not at the attacking limb, but at the teenage girls standing across from her. "Are you going to let me get pulled into the dark? Or will you free me?"

Sarena's hands shook. Elissa pulled her arms around her chest.

The tentacle pulled Lady Marianna's arm closer to the oil. "If my hand touches the oil, another tentacle will reach out. They will pull me in."

Both girls looked at each other, doe-eyed and pale-faced.

"Do something."

Elissa ran around the well, grabbing Lady Marianna by the waist. "I'll help. Pull back, my lady."

"Why should I? This is your test."

Sarena climbed on the edge of the well. She opened her hands and curled her fingers. Reaching forward, the dark-haired girl plunged her nails into the tentacle's rubbery skin. Purple blood rushed out of the deepest wounds, staining the girl's hands.

"Hurry." Lady Marianna's arm inched closer to the oil. "I don't have long."

Elissa braced her feet against the well and pushed against Lady Marianna's abdomen. "Rip it apart," the blonde said.

Closing her fingers, Sarena pulled her arms apart. She held the tentacle tighter, enough that her muscles started to ache.

Elissa slipped, falling on her face.

Lady Marianna scooted forward.

The tentacle tightened around the lady's arm, dragging her close to the darkness.

Sarena screamed. Her grip came loose. Purple blood sprayed all over her face as she tumbled to the side. A wad of flesh still wriggled in her hand.

A string of words echoed through the room. Sarena could not understand the words. Lightning surged in Lady Marianna's free hand as she flattened her fingers. Sweeping her hand once, a barrage of sparks streamed through the air.

A gurgling howl pierced the electrical discharge. Sarena gripped her ears to block out the pain.

Lady Marianna tossed a wounded tentacle to the floor. "This is what we're fighting, girls." The tentacle flopped a few times and sizzled in the dry light. "You both should remember that."

***

The witch stared at the creature before her. His arms coiled like long serpents. The whips around him stretched with a prehensile urgency.

"Your mistress." Sarena heaved air into her remaining lung. "She's a dweller."

"She is more. Far beyond dweller or human."

"Shed your armor." A glimmer of blue surrounded Sarena and her staff. "Show me."

"It is my place to prepare the way."

A whip slammed downward. The witch rolled back. She swung her staff, breaking the whip's skin.

"She wills me to crush you to the precipice." Hobbling, the emissary darted toward Sarena. His tendril-arms whirled through the space between them.

Water splashed out of the fountain. A beam of light drew Joseph back from the dark.

The Legionnaire rushed forward, his lips parted in a hiss. A last glob of spit tumbled out of his mouth as he launched himself at the emissary. When his body ran low on strength, he did not stop to breathe. His sword slashes slowed for a moment. Then stopped.

Both of the emissary's tendril-arms fell slack, drooping onto the surface. "I regenerate. You restore. This place binds both together. Why would you resist?"

***

At the foot of the Dweller Temple, Sarena ran. She'd been in three of the enemy strongholds before, but never one so large.

Her feet couldn't take her outside fast enough.

Rumbling erupted from behind her, then all around her. The growling beast under her feet had already awakened, enraged by the absence of the Black

Pearl in the witch's right hand.

She found the earth-carved steps her Order used when they built the temple within the expansive cave. Before it sank into the dark. Before it was consumed by the other world.

The front of the temple exploded. A chunk of exterior stairs soared over Sarena's head before smashing into the carved path.

Skidding to a stop, Sarena looked ahead and behind. No path, aside from the one leading back to the temple.

Absolute shadow faded as the slithering mass slapped reptilian claws on the broken surface of the pyramid. Emerging in the faint purple glow, the dragon roared. Then it bared a second set of jaws and roared once more. Dozens of dweller tentacles outlined the dragon's mouth like a set of deranged whiskers. The monster's eyes blazed with a black so dark, it made Sarena vomit.

Her hand thrust into her satchel. She needed to escape but lacked the means to fight a dragon, let along survive the experience. Shifting her fingers back and forth, the witch could only shake her head.

She hadn't packed her Binding Barb. Or she'd lost it. Either way, there would be no escape from the dwellers.

Oil seeped from the stones beneath her.

Their beast would destroy her or they would rip her into nothingness. Instead of taking the Black Pearl for her sisters, Sarena had become a trophy for her enemies.

Oily wings flapped in the air. The dweller dragon stomped forward. Even without looking, it knew where to find the witch.

Overhead, the cavern cracked. Sunlight spilled around Sarena. The oil under her feet retreated.

Sunbeams burst through, breaking a deeper wound above her. A dozen Legionnaires swooped from above, plunging into the dragon's flesh. The beast howled through the blood and bile erupting from its mouth.

"Hey," a voice shouted from above. A compact beam of light shot down from the crack, striking a few steps from Sarena. Another witch scaled down the condensed beam of light, her wide-brimmed hat flopping in the air. Elissa landed and smiled. "I haven't forgotten you."

Sarena bumped the palm of her hand against the blonde witch's arm, playfully shoving her away. "I wouldn't let you forget," Sarena said.

Spinning the wide polearm in her hand, Elissa asked, "Shall we slay our demons?"

***

No witch would swoop from the heavens to save Sarena this time. She shook her head, struggling to fathom what the emissary had said.

"Are you a dweller?"

A repetitious noise—almost a laugh—rumbled from the emissary's mouth. "No. Nor is She."

Joseph rose again. His beady eyes locked onto the one defiler who bothered to speak. The Legionnaire thrust Night's Edge forward. The onyx blade passed through the emissary's chest.

One tendril arm wrapped around Joseph's neck. The other snapped around the man's torso. Both limbs tightened and pulled.

"If I remove your head," the emissary asked, "will you return?"

Joseph grinned, showing a gap that had formed between some of his teeth. "Twice a day, you shall find greater strength."

Some of the tension left the emissary's limbs. "Strength in what?"

Sarena glanced to the side, beyond the sunlit outline of the deformed city of Siken. The last glow of the last sun drifted toward the horizon.

And then the suns had all passed into night.

From the emissary's chest, another sun rose, this one pale and etched with darkness. A trace of flame ran over Night's Edge. Then a bolt of lightning, a breath of frost. But the glow of the sun lit strongest of all.

The witch lifted her staff and took aim, but the intensity of Joseph's sword was more than Sarena's eyes could stand.

Within the surge of power, the emissary flailed into a high-pitched scream.

Bone cracked in the growing dusk. Skin and meat tore apart.

The body of a cursed Legionnaire fell. His head dropped and bounced before rolling off into the defiled city.

Rage and disbelief burned in Sarena's eyes. She leveled her weapon at the emissary. But the emissary's body fell limp as well. Night's Edge stayed wedged within the defiler's chest. The wound bubbled with a winter's chill, a gleam of sunlight, and a fading spark of electricity.

The witch took a step forward. Her eyes kept the emissary in sight. She refused to fall victim to a ruse.

In a whisper, Armie asked, "Is it dead?"

She had never encountered anything like the emissary before. Since he'd emerged from the wall, it could be bound to him.

Sarena thrust her staff forward. An azure beam ripped through the emissary's lower torso. Purple and black ooze bubbled out of the wound.

"And the Legionnaire?"

Hearing the priest's question, the witch knelt beside her strained comrade. Without a head, Joseph should have burst into flakes and been restored by the curse.

Sarena prodded the tendril arms away from Joseph's body and rolled him on his side. Dark toned dust spilled out of his open neck. His armor had degraded to barely useful segments.

On his back, several scratches tore through the circular mark. Within each wound, a thin line of red approached the surface but didn't spill out.

A red blister rose from one of the scratches. The other lines of red grew thinner and faded into their wounds.

Sarena placed a hand on the Legionnaire's chest, then leaned over him as time caught up with the fighter's curse.

The witch shifted back. Turning, she said, "It's not over."

Oil seeped out of the emissary's wounds. The shadowy liquid bubbled for a moment.

"What is that?"

"Dweller oil," Sarena said. "For something that isn't a dweller, he had a lot in common with them."

The blister on Joseph's back bulged out, growing as large as a head. Stretching, the blister's skin thickened close to the same size as a neck.

Armie jumped forward, shoving his knife through the bulk of the blister. The skin went limp and the blood within drooled onto the Legionnaire's body. He met Sarena's eyes. "I don't think we should stay here."

She licked her lips. "I think you're right."

***

Throbbing organs drew Sarena's gaze into the city proper. Nodules within each structure made Siken take on a dull orange glow. Seeing the shade made the witch scowl. Her stomach twisted into a knot, threatening to expel its contents.

Beside her, the priest asked the too obvious question. "How do we get down?"

If Sarena could remember all her spells, she would have called upon a beam of light to repel down with. But the phrases were in too many pieces. If she could remember, there was another problem: the suns had already set.

"Does the city want us here," Sarena asked, "or does it want something else?"

"What else could it want?"

She looked back at the dull outline of the valley below. Night had already eclipsed the swamp in shadow. The crevasse where they'd found Joseph was all but invisible to start with. And the village of refugees?

There were no fires on the horizon, not even the sign of a torch. It would be wise to stay hidden, but Chaz didn't seem the type to focus on how to remain unseen. Perhaps they'd made up a great deal of ground.

Perhaps not.

"I'm a fool." Sarena shook her head.

"You've gotten us this far."

"I know."

She walked back to the fountain. The water still glistened with sunlight, even as night settled in. Putting a hand above the surface of the water, the witch closed her eyes. "I wish to see. Open the gates to glimpse past."

The water rippled under her hand, then grew still once more.

"No. That's not it." She bit her lip while rubbing her fingertips together. "That was wrong, but I haven't forgotten."

"Forgotten what?" Armie asked. "I don't understand."

"I'm looking for a way down." There was more, but she didn't let herself think it.

"A scrying spell?"

"Yes." She held her hand over the water once again, closing her eyes. "I wish to see." That phrase was correct, otherwise, the water would never have moved before. Open the gates to glimpse…" "Past" was the wrong word, but it was close. "…beyond."

Her eyes snapped open, her hand was sheathed in a layer of rippling gold.

She lifted her hand and saw a Sunlit witch lifting an onyx-bladed sword, thrusting it into the wall. Blood rushed from the wound fast enough to erode the wall into a series of stones she could jump down without dying.

As her fingers relaxed, her gaze shifted down, pulling farther away. Outside of the valley, Chaz and the other filth-covered refugees fought a horde of defilers. Dozens of crabs followed by just as many wisps. The emissary—or was it a different emissary—led a legion of mutated Sikens out of another nydal worm.

Moving even higher, she watched the fleshy streets of the city ooze throughout the valley. The mass pulled cursed amalgamations from their pits, setting them loose to kill anyone in their path. Nydals burrowed outward, expanding the living city to cover every part of the landscape. Forests became giant strands of hair, town wells became glossy eyes. Armies raised barricades against defiler hordes, only for their spouses to mutate and attack from behind.

Volcanoes became lungs. Mountains nursed fusions the witch could not fathom. Oceans grew crimson skins, gestating the emissary's mistress deep inside.

When the fleshy bulb hatched, the world would be gone.

Only Lila would remain.

Lila.

No longer a corpse lying on a field of ruins and snow, but it was Lila all the same.

Except her eyes were purple and black globes, lacking any iris or pupil. The eyes of a dweller.

Sarena snapped her hand and eyes shut, allowing the spell to fade.

Behind her, the priest spoke. "What did you see?"

"A dead friend at the end of the world. And I'm about to make it happen."

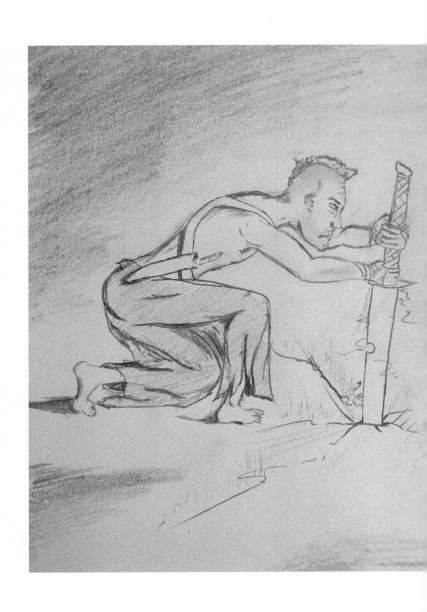

TO BIRTH THE APOCALYPSE

Armie shook his head. "How can you make the end of the world happen?"

Sarena stepped away from the fountain. When she crouched to pick up Night's Edge, she looked at the priest. "When Lotac saw the curse, I think he saw me." She picked up the sword.

"That makes no sense."

"Says the man who used Catechism teachings to throw me into a pit."

The priest reached toward Sarena. "Wait. What did you see?"

Sarena turned the point of Night's Edge at Armie. "I plunged this weapon into the wall, breaking enough of it to make a way in. That also lets them out."

"They can get out whenever they please."

"Maybe that's the trick. Maybe only a few of them can get out." The witch walked past the whip stumps. Only a thin line of light marked the distant horizon.

"If you know this for certain, why let them out? Is the Sanctum that important to you?"

Sarena touched the head of her staff to Night's Edge, washing her azure power over the onyx blade. "One of my sisters is down there. She's the one the emissary kept talking about."

"Another cursed witch?"

The witch shook her head. "Not cursed. Dead."

"Then how can she be down there?"

"That is the question," Sarena said. "Now you know why I have to go."

***

When Sarena first met Lila, they both appeared in front of dweller gateway. Oil had splattered a ruined archway within viewing distance of the Emperor's Coastal Palace. Overhead, the sky shifted from a sunless purple into pure night.

The witches bowed to each other, though neither could speak. The magic Lady Marianna used to draw others across worlds lacked the ability to materialize their complete bodies. Only a similar form made purely of photons could make the journey.

Unlike others who they'd aided, Lady Marianna wore a circlet that made her audible to both of them. "Your purpose here is to observe and report. This world is forfeit, but we can learn much from what the dwellers have done here. Now go."

Both witches bowed and approached the gateway. A swirling mist drifted around the outer barrier. Faces belonging to those slain in this world screamed from the swirls. One mouth stretched into a noiseless shriek before Sarena touched the mist. A ripple of air pushed the expressions away, widening the eye of the localized storm.

She stepped through, seeing only shadows leading into a tunnel bored from the earth itself. There were no stairs, as the dwellers had no feet, not in the human sense of the word.

A gust of air pushed Sarena from behind. The shimmering outline took on a subtle glow as Lila grew closer.

The mists locked together, sealing the witches within the shadowed realm.

Sarena waved her fingers, beckoning Lila to follow her downward. Ahead—far ahead—a dull speck of purple marked their destination.

Every time Sarena saw a dweller realm, she couldn't understand how such a purple glow could grow in absolute darkness. It was not fire, it possessed no heat, yet it was always there, a constant beacon.

From time to time, she would look back to make sure Lila was still with her. The young witch had a habit of looking up at the tunnel ceiling or peeking into small holes. If Sarena could, she would have tied a rope around her companion to pull her along.

The ramp cut off in the tunnel, replacing half the floor with an open chasm. Purple luminescence traced a line deep in the gap, but neither witch wanted to explore the dweller realm in such a method.

When the tunnel widened into the courtyard of a subterranean city, Sarena knew they were on the right path. Stalactites and stalagmites poked out from the floor and ceiling. Past those, a dozen domed buildings lay wrapped in a thick mist and a sheen of purple. Pools of dweller oil scattered throughout the courtyard, though none bubbled with an immediate threat.

Lila, gazing at the distant city, walked past Sarena. The young witch's mouth fell open in awe of the hidden lair poking into at least a few worlds. She stopped just short of an oil pool and crouched.

The young witch pulled back her sleeve and spread her fingers just above the pool.

Sarena filled her staff with all her excess power. The girl was about to make the most classic mistake.

If she could call out to Lila and warn her —

But the dweller's tentacle snapped upward, snagging Lila's exposed arm. The young witch thrust her spear into the pool, driving the dweller to the surface.

The creature's glossy eyes locked onto Lila. Five more tentacles snapped out of the black sludge, splattering the pristine cave floor. The appendages battered Lila's ethereal form, knocking the young witch's spear away.

Sarena shifted her staff, blasting the dweller's thick, clear-skinned torso. The creature reeled back, tossing its head around. If she were actually present, Sarena had no doubt she would be crippled by the dweller's wail.

Pulling down, the dweller lashed Lila's legs and waist. The young witch lost her footing, leaving her unable to resist falling into the pool of oil.

Sarena skidded to a stop just short of the pool. Her young charge was gone, along with the attacker. She prayed Lila would be able to return to her body quickly rather than enduring whatever waited in the dweller's depths.

***

Armie raised his hands in a submissive gesture. "Let's talk about this. We don't know anything that's going to happen?"

The witch let her arms fall slack at her sides. Both of the weapons she carried scraped over the surface of the wall.

"Before the curse, I worked with a young witch. She saw things no one had ever seen before. She might still be the only one. Somehow, she is in that city. She's been calling my name ever since someone from your group first shot me in the eye."

Several screeches ripped through the night sky.

"I don't know what's happened, but the only way to stop it is to go forward."

"I share that goal with you, witch—"

"Then why stop me?"

"Because you speak of the world's end. What sense is there in dooming the world to answer a small question?"

Sarena's mouth tightened. "You never had to fight the dwellers."

"Perhaps not. But I fight these defilers with you now."

"They co-opt flesh to build their armies. I have seen that now."

The priest pointed at the surface between them. "Are they truly trapped in these walls?"

"I have seen them escape."

"As a certainty?"

Her lips parted, but the affirmation never arrived. The witch looked down into the city as more spots of luminescence dotted the landscape. "I saw how I would destroy much of this wall, then how many of them marched outward."

"Many have already marched outward."

"Armies?" the witch asked. "A hundred legions? A billion companies? It's enough to give them the world."

"Yet they have left these walls before."

The witch clanged the base of her staff against the surface. "Why have these walls to begin with?"

Armie shrugged. "To defend themselves?"

"Maybe." Sarena sent a glance over her shoulder. When would a crab, a wisp, or something worse come looking for them? "I wonder if it is like the body. Our skin is the wall build to hold everything together. Our organs and fluids constantly move inside."

"If that's true, then breaking the wall would kill them."

She shook her head. "We've already seen what their blood will do to anything it comes in contact with. The slopes leading toward the city are dead. You know how cruel the swamp was."

The priest stood silent for a moment, rubbing his fingers against the palm of his right hand. "Do you think this city has enough blood to cause the end of times?"

"Directly? No. But I think it can corrupt enough that it will set off a chain reaction."

"Then it comes to one act to determine the fate of the world."

Sarena nodded. "That's what I've been saying."

"Then allow me to counter your conclusion," Armie said. "Let me strike the wall."

"I don't think you're strong enough—"

"Which is why I should do it." The priest moved toward the witch, his movements lacked any tension. "If I do it, the wall might break, but not crumble. The barrier would still restrain the blood flowing from the wall."

***

"I can hold them off," Lila said, looking down from the tower of the Northern Keep.

The Legion of Flame, driven mad from their curse, marched upon the last bastion of the Sunlit Order in the region. A long dusk fell onto the snow-crusted mountain pass.

"This isn't a game," Sarena said.

"I know better than to look into any pools of dweller oil," the young witch said. "We need to make them stop long enough for the new recruits to charge at them."

Elissa nodded. "I didn't expect the squad posted here to be so fresh."

"None of them have much experience in war." Sarena shook her head. "A neophyte and a bunch of reservists trying to take on the most well-trained legion of modern times."

"I know better now," Lila said. "I've been preparing some new spells. I can speak into their minds and they'll obey me."

Sarena sat on the floor, covering her face with both hands.

Lila stood taller. Her voice remained even as she spoke. "The Scroll of Jeanne the Pale was never forbidden. It's difficult, but I've been working with it. If I can't connect to their minds, then we can use the side effect to our advantage."

Sarena remembered the one time she read The Scroll. She trembled at the thought of causing a creature's brain to ignite in flames.

"It's worth a shot," Elissa said. She patted Sarena's shoulder. "Don't be so down about this. You and I both learned a lot since the first time we saw a pool of dweller oil."

The dark-haired witch exhaled slowly before she nodded. "You've been stronger these past few months." Sarena allowed herself to smile as she faced her younger counterpart. "Smarter too."

Lila grinned. "You're just saying that because I pulled you out of that dweller temple."

"A-hem!" Elissa frowned. "I recall having to pull both of you out of that particular temple."

"But," Sarena said, "Lila did hold off six dwellers before the Legion swept in."

"It would have been more if my echo didn't get killed."

Sarena offered the young witch a tiny smile. "You're stronger than you know," Sarena said in a whisper. Laughing for an instant, she spoke louder. "Don't let it go to your head."

Lila timidly smirked. "Too late."

***

Armie held out his right hand. "Will you let me do it?"

In that moment, Night's Edge lifted with ease. The light-weight tip tended to flow upward, caught in the slightest breeze. Sarena whispered to herself. "I see. That's how he knew." The witch turned to her last ally. "It seems like Night's Edge likes your idea."

The sword's handle sizzled between her fingers.

"Be careful," Sarena said, holding the weapon laterally. "Night's Edge is Princess-kissed."

He nodded. "I remember you and Legionnaire Armand discussing that earlier." The priest put his hand on the handle.

Without letting go of the sword, Sarena asked, "Do you know what that means?"

The priest paused for a moment. "I think so."

"You swore to serve Lotac, but this weapon has been in the presence of the Sky Lord's own granddaughter, the Lady Marianna."

Armie's eyes widened and his hand pulled back.

Sarena pushed the priest's hand back onto the handle. "Just because she pledged herself to the Sunlit Order doesn't mean she stopped being a Princess." The witch laughed. "If I mentioned it when she was around, Lady Marianna would slap me. You don't know a sting like being slapped in the mouth by a Princess."

The priest shifted his bandaged hand. "I suppose being scolded by a member of the divine bloodline would be quite the experience."

Sarena let go of the sword and Armie's hand. "It stung like nothing before or since. Not even that sludge in the swamp."

As the witch stepped away, she saw an ellipse glow in the center of the sword. The shape was incomplete on the long ends thanks to a subtle gap lined with a few glowing marks.

The priest's face went blank. "I… I never thought…"

"That Princess-kissed was a literal term? If I hadn't seen her do it with another sword, I would have doubted it myself."

Skittering echoed from the shadows around them. Tiny scrapes told Sarena of a hundred little limbs creeping toward her and Armie en masse. All that remained was for the fight to begin again.

"If you're going to do it," the witch said, empowering her staff, "you should strike now."

She turned away, not knowing what defilers were coming. She'd already been thrown into slumber by one cluster, skewered with infection by another.

Limbs as thin as reeds stepped from the shadows, stalking on a web-shaped path. Canine growls echoed above each arachnid step.

"I call upon the Final Flame," she whispered. The phrases aligned with ease, too much for a spell that would rip her apart from the inside. "Taste the fury burning within me." Tongues of blue fire rushed from the head of her staff and curled around her. She noticed the spindly legs holding up gaunt dog bodies. One of the approaching beasts had the head of a bloodied bird instead of a canine.

Behind Sarena, Armie cried out with fury. The witch turned for an instant as the priest raised Night's Edge. Air froze around the blade. Lightning crackled from the icy cloud, lighting thin trails of ash on the cutting edge. The elements swirled around Armie's body. His bandaged hand exploded with limp tendrils, all falling dead with shock and smoke.

The priest screamed louder as the wind rushed at the surface of the wall.

Night's Edge plunged into the crisp flesh of the wall. Blood spurted upward as cracks of light ate through the barrier. Embers rushed from the growing fissures, catching in Armie's robes. As he lit into flame, so did the wall. When his body transformed into a gleaming pyre, the wall exploded.

Sarena flew backward, smashing against the surface twice.

A thousand dog and bird beasts cried out in the newborn night.

THE EMBEDDED QUEEN

Lingering under the blanket of night, Sarena lifted her head. Smoke still rippled around her. Ash flakes drifted around the cracked wall. Trickles of blood made the ruptured edges damp.

The scent of roasted hair tugged at her nasal passages, refusing to let go. Even as she covered her face, the witch found Armie again and again.

Below, the defiler flesh of Siken continued rushing and churning. Each body ran about in a perfect pattern, drifting from one neighborhood to the next. Sarena wondered if the captured people were forced to act like building blocks of a larger body.

She spat to the side, noting again the broken chunks of the fountain she'd built.

Turning away, she found the reason for her dismissal.

Night's Edge, the onyx blade of Joseph Armand, lay in a mound of shards. A hand of fire-whipped bones still gripped the fallen handle.

Sarena touched the sword's hilt. "This is why you never blessed our weapons," the witch said to her absent mistress. "If we willfully use such power against our own, we would be…" Rather than hear herself admit she'd been cast out, Sarena fell forward.

Her left hand gripped the jagged edge of the wall. Even with cracks to navigate downward, Sarena knew it would be a long climb.

She moved slowly, knowing that it was not simply a wall she climbed down. It was a barrier bound to her fallen sister Lila.

***

After the rest of the cursed left the Northern Keep in smoking ruins, Sarena turned back. Those cast into death remained slain and unmoving.

The witch walked among the fallen, looking once more for Lila. Snow crunched under Sarena's feet. Blood-soaked mud opened small gaps in the field of white.

Sarena saw a young woman's body and lunged at the fallen earth. When the witch rolled the corpse, she wailed, smashing her fist into the ground.

It wasn't Lila, but a servant girl from the keep. She didn't even have a weapon.

She kept moving across the battlefield, turning over corpses. The masked woman had abandoned the young witch, refusing to mark her.

From the Iceblood Gate, someone waved their arms and called out.

Sarena couldn't make out the sound.

The witch turned over more bodies, but could not find Elissa or Lila. The only female bodies present belonged to fallen soldiers. None had Lila's full cheeks or her idealistic charm.

"Sarena."

She looked up. The approaching figure called her name once more. Blond hair trailed out behind the woman.

"Elissa?"

The blonde witch approached, holding the brim of her wide-brimmed hat. "Lila's not here."

Sarena rose. "I can find her. Help me." She drifted to another corner of the battlefield, turning over corpses.

"She isn't here, Sarena. She's gone."

"They didn't curse her."

"She's not here."

The same refrain echoed from the blonde, no matter how much Sarena wanted to find Lila. Finally, Sarena asked, "If she's not here, where is she?"

***

The streets of Siken swelled with a spongy layer shifting between a deep purple and shadowy gray. Veins webbed through the layer, pulsing life through the defiled city.

Muscle grew over the buildings. Smaller huts expanded in one moment, contracted the next. All shifted with the same rhythm, in and out, in and out. Between the huts, larger structures had been built with armored carapaces. Slender openings allowed one defiler to pass at a time.

In and out. In and out.

A few scattered citizens of Siken emerged from the larger structures. All nude, all clad in leathery lizard-skin. Their steps left moist footprints, which absorbed into the spongy streets after lingering a few moments.

Sarena hunched low, trying to not press the base of her staff into the soft streets. She peeked around the bulging huts, moving only when she thought the path was clear.

The witch followed a defiled citizen as they carried a fleshy sac full of bright orange liquid. Even when the street sloped downward toward the central structure, the defiler didn't spill a single drop. Another defiler approached the first from the opposite direction. Neither spoke, only drifting a step to the side just before colliding.

The new defiler turned her head toward Sarena but did not stop. Even without eyes, she was sure the beast could still see.

Twice the first defiler turned with Sarena still in pursuit. He carried his parcel to the edge of an earthen pool. Twenty defilers crouched at the edge of the glowing bowl of crimson liquid.

Sarena watched the first defiler as he stepped to the edge of the pool and squatted. A fleshy probe rose from the ground, pressing into his back. The liquid in his sac shifted as it began to drain.

Another defiler rose. A deflated sac hung from his abdomen and a probe dangled from his spine. He walked away from the pool, so Sarena followed him, hoping he might go further into the city.

He walked the streets along the perimeter. A female approached him and they both stepped to the side, just like the pair Sarena watched before. This female had eyes but didn't regard the witch as she passed.

In time, the defiler walked into a long building bound to the earth by an alternating sequence of ribs. He stopped at the edge of a wide opening marked with a ring of dissimilar barbs. Several of the natural hooks reached outward, pressing into the defiler. His muscles drained, leaving him with nothing more than tight skin and spindly bones. Yet he marched on, leaving the building behind.

Sarena peered into the opening for a moment. Threads of mucus dripped from the shadowy ceiling, reminding her of the worm she'd slain at the edge of the village.

With the defiler walking toward the center of the city, the witch dashed to catch up. She glanced up and to her right, trying to judge the height of the tower in the center of the city. The structure's windows breathed like the huts she'd already passed. Each exhale spewed a blackened mist into the air. Sarena wanted to get closer, sure that Lila had to be trapped somewhere within the highest of Siken's buildings.

Yet no sentries had stopped her. The defiled citizens barely cared when she passed by.

***

Lila raced into the dweller nest ahead of the others. The oil-soaked walls of the tall hallway gave little reassurance. Sarena feared they would be too late, though she hadn't voiced her concern, even to Elissa.

Two of the tentacled beasts appeared from the intersection ahead. One scurried low, rushing toward Lila. The other slapped its limbs against the walls, bracing itself as it dashed overhead.

Sarena blasted downward, while her blonde counterpart jumped ahead with her bardiche, cleaving the dweller with the long polearm.

Lila drew her wand, flicking the tip at the dweller overhead. A glowing speck zoomed upward before expanding into an instant of daylight. The light set the high dweller ablaze, while the lower creature smoldered in the false sunbeams.

"Solar flare," Lila said with a smile.

They dashed toward the intersection, all quietly hoping to find Lady Marianna in time.

Their mistress lay on a drab altar, bound with ropes and lathered in dweller oil. Her left eye and cheek had turned black and blue from abuse. She groaned as the witches entered the chamber.

Sarena looked around the room, even glancing at the shadow-wrapped ceiling. "I can't believe they left her alone."

"They could be back." Elissa looked over the rope coiled around Marianna's left arm. The blonde witch started cutting the cord with a slender knife. "We'll have you out soon, Lady."

Marianna coughed. Spittle flew from her mouth. "Leave me."

Lila loosened the opposite arm. "Don't worry. You're safe now."

"No." Lady Marianna's voice grew coarse with every cough. "Iriyatha killed the dwellers here. She told me to join her, but I refused."

Frowning, Elissa whispered to Sarena. "She's delirious."

"Could they have drugged her?"

The Lady grew louder again. "The Legion of Flame marches to the Northern Keep. I told her and still she hounded me. The Legion marches into the grasp of the most traitorous devils." She snapped a hand over Lila's arm. "You have to stop her, Lila. Leave this place." Lady Marianna stared at Sarena. "Hurry, before its too late."

Sarena nodded. "We will, my Lady."

"I think you're right, Sarena." Elissa put her knife away. "They must have drugged her. But if she told them that…"

Scowling, Sarena looked across the altar. "Lila. We're leaving."

The young witch shook her head. "What?"

Elissa said, "Go. I'll finish things here."

Sarena extended her hand and approached the door. "Come on, Lila."

Lila stepped away from the altar with a sigh. She took Sarena's hand and they both left the chamber.

The echoes of Lady Marianna crept behind them.

***

Siken grew darker, lit only by the coming and going of luminous fluids. The central tower loomed higher, speckled with bits of light.

Despite all their moving, the defiled citizens made no noise.

Distant screams woke Sarena from her half-asleep nightmare. Her feet swept her forward, just as she wished she'd learned a spell to increase her speed. She dashed into plaza dominated by a wide, luminous pool. Defilers squatted along its edge. Beyond, crabs pulled mud-covered villagers toward a tan building shaped like a wide teardrop.

Seven steps led toward a dais nested inside a series of man-sized tusks. Massive green eyes looked out in four directions. A gasping mouth opened wide above the eyes.

Horns burst up from the nearest street, all draining luminous fluid from the closest pool.

The same masculine scream cried out once more. Nested within the line of crabs, Chaz twitched. His arms spasmed, reminding Sarena of her vision of the village's downfall.

Pulling him by the waist, the crab scurried up the steps of the building. Another mouth opened on the dais and the crab crawled inside.

With so much focus on the line of villagers, the witch bumped into a defiled man, spilling his fluid sac onto the street.

Every defiler made a low, ceaseless moan. The buildings joined in the tone, just as the teardrop-shape turned its eyes toward Sarena.

A hundred hisses screeched around her. Pores opened in the street, unleashing waves of spider-legged hairless rats. Nearby defilers stretched their arms, stretching their sacs into a webbing of skin.

Sarena imbued her staff, swinging it like a mace. Blue sparks flickered around her as she struck the defiler she'd collided with. The man ruptured into a torn bag of skin and meat.

Three of the rats jumped on her legs. She stomped on the spongy surface, trying to loosen them, but their feet pierced her skin as they climbed.

More defilers lumbered toward her. Each floppy step made them move faster.

Sarena smashed the end of her staff into her leg, popping two of the rats open. Their bodies spilled down her own.

On the other side of the pool, leathery tendrils coiled around Chaz, making him sink into the side of the building. The streams of fluid quickened, spewing streams of nightmare afterbirth.

A defiler grabbed Sarena from behind. She snapped her head back, forcing the creature backward. Another defiler grabbed her staff, draping its wet skin over the shaft. Hot steam rose from the witch's weapon.

Sarena punched the defiler ahead of her. Sparks of blue burned the mutated man as he collapsed.

The liquid on the staff melted the shaft, snapping it in half.

The witch swung the lower end, knocking off the last rat. Seeing the imbued power fade, she tossed it at the growing swarm. Several vermin exploded, but the street bubbled as well.

Glowing liquid poured into the teardrop building's mouth. Regurgitating, a darker trail of fluid poured over its surface, splattering on the dais.

A drop fell from Sarena's weapon, burning instantly into her right foot. Her boot smoked. She hobbled toward the pool, knowing how to use it as a weapon.

More defilers rose, swiftly shambling toward her.

Sarena clenched her teeth, feeling blood seep from her gums. Her eyes burned as she looked at the noxious pool. Azure light grew from the remaining half of her staff, enough where she could see her own shadow on the rats swarming her way.

She thought of the cannon that struck the side of the Northern Keep.

She felt Night's Edge pierce the back of her mouth.

She saw Lila's lifeless eyes lying in the snow.

The light hurled from her in an arc, thrashing against the pool.

Green and fire ripped through the air, knocking Sarena off her feet, smashing her backward.

***

A misty morning obscured Sarena's view of the Skyborn Range. Lila used the last of their campfire to heat a pan with a small portion of bread. Elissa sat in the distance with her back to the others, cleaning the blade of her bardiche.

Once she took a swig from her canteen, Sarena held it out for the younger witch. "When she finishes with that, she'll want to go."

Lila took the water, giving only a faint smile. "Do you think we should go to the Northern Keep?"

"It doesn't matter if I think we should. We'll end up there anyway."

"Not if we don't go." The younger witch took a sip from the canteen, then passed it back.

"Sometimes places call to us. We can deny them all we want, but events will push us there all the same."

Lila took her pan from the fire. "Then we don't have any real choice in what happens." She lifted the bread with two fingers and tore it in half.

"We always have a choice. How we choose to take things on is as important as the battle itself."

The younger witch passed half of her bread to Sarena. "Then we'll fight the dwellers there."

"It's not always the dwellers," Sarena said. Using her teeth, she tore a strip off the bread and swallowed it. After taking a drink, she said, "And it's not always a battle in the sense of warfare. The real fight is within, the fight we will always face alone."

Giggling, Lila said, "I'll never have that problem."

Sarena's eyes widened. "We all have to face ourselves eventually."

"True, but you always have my back."

Shaking her head, the witch capped her canteen while Elissa kept to her cleaning.

***

Sarena expected to wake in the realm of darkness, left to reassemble her mind and body, leaving stray pieces of her psyche for the abyss.

Instead, there was light and smoke.

Her right leg lay twisted and charred. Spotted burns opened holes in her ragged dress.

Around her, the living city twitched. Fleshy clumps lay around the scorched ruins of the pool, bodies that had once been defilers and people before that.

Still gripping the top of her staff, the witch pushed herself up to a seated position. Her burned leg refused to bend. She couldn't tell the difference between her leg and her boot, not by sight or by touch.

Dropping the melted head of her staff, Sarena pushed her twisted fingers against her thigh. Ashen scales crumbled under her fingertips. Parting her lips, Sarena murmured the phrases to heal her muscles. She let out a little whimper and slumped forward. Her eyes flooded with tears.

A moment later, she watched her leg bend a little. With muscles that looked less like barren trees, the witch stood up. Hands at her sides, she swayed to hold her balance.

Still lit with bioluminescent specks, the central tower drew Sarena's attention. She hobbled forward, one clumsy step after another.

The ground crumbled under pressure from her feet. Clumps of ash, dried mucus, and gravel marked every step and long stretches where Sarena dragged her leg.

She glanced to the side, watching the ashen mound and its fallen tusks. Glimmering flakes drifted as the burnt husk crumbled. As she turned back to the central tower, a mumbled voice rolled out of the ruins.

"Filthy witch." The witch recalled the voice. She hadn't expected Chaz to become cognizant again. "Knew you was nothin. But leather."

Sarena shook her head and walked on.

"Don't walk away now." Chaz hacked several times, choking as he spat out the words. "Gonna leave me to die. Shoulda ground you to paste."

A dry gasp was broken a sound the witch imagined was vomit. She didn't bother stopping.

"Pulled that arrow from your eye." Another sound ruptured from his body, but Sarena didn't guess which part. "Ain't nothin but a rotted carcass. Gonna kill us all."

She kept walking onward, letting her right leg drag a little longer than before.

"Y'hear me, witch." Chaz coughed. "Do ya?"

If Sarena heard anything through the filthy man's cries and rambling, she made no sign of it. Her legs dragged over the broken surface as she walked down the slope leading toward the central tower.

***

Nothing approached her as she trekked further into the core of Siken. The outer walls of the central tower pulsed like a beating heart, though Sarena saw no blood, be it red or luminous yellow. None of the defiled population approached. Looking back, the witch saw none of the citizens trailing about their appointed tasks.

She stopped, wishing for the phrase to create the corona of protective bolts above her head. Her fingers shook in front of her, trembling with the loss of her tools.

All she could think of was an emerald blossom in her satchel. Biting the petals off a plant seemed too much a chore for her. The clump of plucked roots tumbled from her hand and rolled toward a pulsing gateway. The last gleaming petal caught under the withered slug that remained of her foot and boot.

Two flaps of skin beat like the valves of a heart. Their edges overlapped for an instant before tearing apart once more.

A long exhale, the first she could remember since climbing down, pushed past her lips, cracking both in the center. "I'm here. And you know it. You can let me in or I can stand here."

The flaps whipped open, rippling in a wind Sarena could not feel.

With darkness ahead, she stepped forward.

Veins of gleaming yellow and red webbed over the walls as they rose higher. She looked up, seeing thin windows of skin, visible only with the dimmest of light from the night sky. Pale ribs rose from bare, smooth ground. Not a single grain of dust tumbled inside.

A single snap freed the flaps behind the witch. She turned back out of instinct but saw nothing. No ladder or staircase to climb.

In the center of the smooth floor, Sarena found a triangular opening with smoothed points. The sides of the opening curved inward as well. No light surged up to meet her, not even a single gleam.

***

Through shadow, she fell. Despite the pitch of her abyss, Sarena could still hear the echo of her body speeding past the walls of another pit. Currents pressed against her body, rippling around her until—

Sarena's arm and shoulder collided with a polished floor cloaked in absolute darkness. The tips of her fingers slipped as she tried to push herself back up. Within her shoulder, the bones smashed together, grinding her ability to move into dust. A whimper of pain crept up her throat but lodged under her voice box.

A ripple of dull purple washed over the floor. A low ceiling loomed at the edge of the shadows. No walls bothered revealing themselves.

The crumpled heart within Sarena's chest chugged as the witch pushed herself up. Her palms slapped the floor, frantic to help her rise.

Familiar flapping sounds struck the floor, though she saw no oil. Still, she knew there were tentacles in the darkness around her. Reaching, feeling.

Sarena reached for her coins. As her fingers closed around the empty bag, she remembered the tokens had lost all power, drained by the same forces that once empowered her.

"They betrayed her too." The voice in the shadows was quiet, soft, even feminine.

Sarena wasn't sure it was human.

"Are you her?" the witch asked. "The one in charge?"

"No one is in charge." A solid form pressed on the edge of the shadows. Larger than a person, the shape glided to a stop, arms outstretched, torso extending to the floor. "Elissa could not barter her way into the Sanctum. You could not convince the refugees to free you. I cannot control this body."

A lean tendril whipped out of the dark, snapping like a whip around Sarena's left wrist. She closed her fingers around the limb, pressing her fading strength into her fingernails. Dragging her hand away, the tendril ripped with trails of faint azure trailing behind.

Blood dripped from the torn cord. Red and thick, not the slimy black Sarena knew should be around her.

"Where is Lila, dweller?"

"Yes," the shape said. "Here. Hurt. A dead echo."

The shape glided forward as more tentacles swayed around the central mass. Several defilers stepped forward, their bodies pierced by mucus-covered veins. Among them, a dirty-faced woman scowled as she looked at the witch. Rather than acting, Bea breathed in far too much, her body swelling with each gasp.

At the center of the mass, a chitinous cask dangled from the ceiling, shifting closer to Sarena. Embedded within, a young woman held her arms to her sides, while her legs and the top of her head remained confined in a hardened shell. Her skin, even the skin of her tentacles, shimmered like the carapace of a wet cockroach. Armored plates hooked around her eyes, never letting her stop looking outward.

"Not cursed, but an echo," the woman said. "A mistake."

Sarena stared at the full cheeks of the trapped woman, the slight dimple in her chin. The witch's eyes felt moistened with grief. With the only breath Sarena could manage, she asked, "How?"

"They found her at the Northern Keep. They could not take Lady Marianna. They did not get you or Elissa. They did find her."

"But…" The phrase she wanted couldn't reach Sarena's lips.

"They are capable of more than the Sunlit Order knows. They crawled under the battle. When her body struck the ground, they pushed inside. Nesting."

Sarena's fists closed. Her knees creaked as she stood. Tiny plumes of bright blue pierced the air around her knuckles. If she had the strength, she would have scowled, but all sense of tactics and strategy had abandoned her. "Dweller."

"They are. I," Lila said, "am not." The tentacles pulled behind the cask, leaving the young woman open and exposed. "The story is not done."

In the shadows, soft white light splashed in the air. A trickle filled the air, just as a simple track filled with the clear liquid.

"Drink, if you like."

Hollow in voice, Sarena said, "No."

Without response, Lila continued. "They pulled her into the dark and gestated within her. They touched her thoughts. They knew what she knew, just as they planned to. They did not expect to find the mass waiting in one of their pools. The young within did not know what it could be."

Sarena shook her head in confusion.

"They struggle with your words. She is only an echo. I cannot make it work."

"How many of you are there?"

One of the tentacles swept forward, then the other two. Their tips lifted in a row in front of the witch. "They, you call dwellers. She, you call Lila. And I."

"What are you called?"

Lila's eyes shifted side to side since she could not shake her head. "I am mass. I heal the gaps."

"Heal?" Sarena coughed, toppling forward. "Can't you see what you've done?"

"I've healed it all. Roads. Earth. Sky. Air. Scavengers. Dwellers. Lila. Death. Life. I've healed it all."

The witch spat phlegm as she forced herself to sit up again. "You've perverted it."

"She said 'corrupted.' Hamner said 'defiled.' All are healed in Siken. I am one."

Lifting her head, Sarena asked the only thing that made sense to her. "How many have you killed?"

"None. Some died. Refugees sick, infected. Built nydals to find and heal."

"Plainly." Sarena pressed a fist to her mouth as she coughed. "Speak plainly."

"Trying. Not much echo left. Only moments."

The witch looked around her. Defilers shambled in place, gasping air for Lila to breathe.

Sarena stood in a dweller nest, but they'd stopped attacking her. Every tentacle lay dormant, waiting.

She stared at her dead friend, gazing into strained, pale eyes. "Why haven't you killed me?"

"They hate you. She loves you." Lila sucked in a deep breath. "I need you."

"Why?"

"Heal mass." Lila frowned.

"I thought you did the healing."

Within the cask, the young woman's lips trembled, exposing her serrated teeth. Her head dipped as far forward as she could move. Two drops of moisture fell from her eyes, one from each side, both moving perfectly parallel. "Help her," Lila said.

Smashing her fists against the floor, Sarena screamed at the cask gliding above her. "I don't know what you want."

A rush of color flooded Lila's irises. She gasped, then suddenly winced. "Sarena, I don't have long."

"For what—"

"You said you'd always help me, even though you started disappointed with me. When I touched that pool of dweller oil."

The witch shook her head. Her young friend almost sounded normal.

"I died, but the dwellers kept part of me going, so they could learn from me. They found a pool of healing mass and it fused us."

It became clear. A healing mass with the conquering compulsion of a dweller could consume anything.

"I'm just an echo now," Lila said. "The dweller part of me is growing stronger."

"I can kill it."

Lila narrowed her eyes. "You broke yourself getting here. And there are other nodes."

Sarena gripped the bottom of the cask, dragging herself up. "How do we stop it?"

"Control it. The dweller part can't blot out what can't die."

The witch leaned against the cask, staring at her friend's animated death mask. "Tell me how."

"This structure controls the entire hive, even other nodes. Everything obeys the Embedded Queen."

Sarena slipped forward, her forehead pressing against Lila's. "You have to be kidding."

"It's like that binding trick when we raced. You can lock it in place."

To the side, one of the defilers spoke. "Don't you do it, leather." Bea's filthy face scowled deeper as her hands blindly grabbed at the veins linking her to the cask. "Cut this cord so the monster dies."

"That's what they do," Lila whispered. "There's enough that's still dweller to animate her. It's not total fusion."

Sarena touched the cord between the cask and Bea. The thick leather felt hollow, even aside from its slight bulging. Her fingers closed around the mass.

Bea and Lila both gasped.

"Why is this here?" the witch asked. Her fingers tightened, straining the surface of the cord.

All the defilers gasped, flexing their jaws like fish flopping on dry ground.

Sarena eased her grip, swaying in front of Lila on depleted limbs. "The Legion stabbed you through the chest. They must have hit your lungs."

"Cut me loose," Bea said. "Let that monster suffocate and die."

Ignoring the angered voice, Sarena touched her friend's cheek. Lila's skin was as stiff as a thin sheet of cold metal. "Lila, in my heart, I wish there was another way."

Wet air pushed through the young woman's armored nose. Her mouth opened, trying to breathe through the saws in her mouth.

"I do love you."

The words floated away from Sarena as her remaining power surged into her bony fingers. Pushing into the edges of the cask, the witch whipped her magic around Lila's armor-plated neck. Luminous blood washed over Sarena's hands, stinging her strained skin.

Sarena's stomach clenched, spurting acid up her throat. She and Lila coughed in the same instant, though the latter's made only a tiny, desperate sound. A single hiccup dropped a thick black mass onto the witch's thumb, sliding off a moment later.

Along the floor, the defilers reached up. Their hands flailed at the air as their jaws dangled open. In the same moment, they all fell.

Sarena wished her eyes could cry. If such an act could free her from the blood on her hands or the dead tissue around her fingers. She hung on the front of the cask, dangling in the hope that she could sway to sleep.

But the moment remained.

Inside the witch, she felt the rages of her curse. The violent temper she'd held back surged into her arms. Her mouth opened, releasing every stab of her flesh, every arrow that had pierced her skin. Every wound returned, fueling the memory bursting from Sarena's mouth.

The fanged scar on her back released its bite.

Nothing could draw Lila apart from the confused remnants of dweller flesh and confused healing mass.

As the pain left Sarena, she tightened her grip on Lila's body. The young witch did not belong in a dark pit. She should be in the Sanctum, maybe in a sunny grove of flowers.

First, she had to pull Lila free. Tendrils coiled out of the young witch's back, anchoring her to the cask. A pair of dweller tentacles burst out of Lila's sides, bathing her in a dark slurry of multi-colored blood.

Together, they tumbled back, with Sarena's back slapping against the floor. She gazed up at the shadowed ceiling for an eternity of seconds before rolling over. Crawling toward the font, she untied the laces on her dress.

At the font, Sarena stretched her arm into the liquid. After cupping a little in her hand, she splashed it on Lila. The act of diluting the blood loosened the stains so the witch could wipe her friend clean. It was no royal bath of sacred waters, but she had nothing else to work with.

Braids of frayed hair still looped around Lila's head, giving Sarena one less chore to attend to. The witch winced as she pulled off her dress and draped it over Lila's head. She pulled the roughened cloth down, gently tightening it around Lila's midriff.

Kissing the young witch's forehead, Sarena said, "There is nothing else I can give."

Author's Note for the Complete Edition

Here I am again, revisiting the compiled version of *Scars Of Shadow*.
My love for the game *Dark Souls* is a common thread in my work, but nowhere
more than this story and the larger setting of *The Fanged Circle*. I thought splicing
in some of my enjoyment of the movie *Prometheus* would be a perfectly weird
addition, one I hope you've found some enjoyment in reading.

While this isn't the setting that compels me to write most often, I still
enjoy *Scars Of Shadow*. Sarena's journey has sparks of wonder and a thread of
hope even in the face of friction, adversity, and darkness. Is it inspiring? I don't
know. Maybe, possibly. Much like *Dark Souls*, there's a wealth of difficulty to
overcome—but it can be done.

The original assembly of this story was easy enough. It was my second
pass at releasing something independently. I haven't changed the text of the
story in the four years between releasing the final installment and saving this file.
There are too many other stories for me to write and distribute. I feel it would be
unfair to my Patreon supporters who helped fund the individual installments of
Scars Of Shadow. That's a decision my peers haven't always agreed with, but it's
still my choice—and responsibility.

For this complete edition, I've commissioned a new cover from Alexandra Purtan of Fenix Cover Designs. Every stage of her work has been nearly immaculate, from her initial sketch to the final image gracing the cover. Her version has so much more personality and scope than the image I first used in 2017, which I've left at the start of the text. I'd love it if you looked at Alexandra's work at https://fenixcoverdesigns.com/

I'm still grateful to my friends and fellow writers, just as I'm lucky to have supporters for newer projects, whether they be posted on Patreon or made available through an online retailer.

An extra thanks goes out to Mike Jack Stoumbos for his continued encouragement. Paige Miller did similar with her wonderfully opinionated eye. Michael J. Allen showed me a better way to release stories online to better reach a wider audience. These are just three of a great host of allies I've been fortunate to have in my corner.

I'm even more grateful to you for having spent time with my words and ideas. I invite you to share a review of how *Scars Of Shadow* made you feel. Or you can tell your friends. Or read another tale that's escaped my mind to venture into a wider world. My gratitude will remain intact just for reading my work.

My thanks will never be enough.

-Len Berry
January 19, 2022

Please enjoy this sample from Len Berry's dystopian novel,

VITAMIN F

Bridgett focused her attention on the blonde sitting a few rows to her right instead of the history lecture. Every few minutes, Bridgett made an unconscious turn, getting a view of the elegant young woman. At first, Bridgett couldn't believe the thick, flowing hair falling down the young woman's shoulders. The blonde's shimmering eyes came into view next, along with her soft cheeks. Bridgett stayed fixated on the blonde's face as long as she dared, dreading the idea of her actually looking back.

To her immediate left, Bridgett detected a subtle movement. When Bridgett turned, she saw a girl wearing all black shaking her head. "Pay attention," Delilah whispered.

At the same volume, Bridgett said, "I am."

The other girl rolled her eyes in response.

"How many students are there at this university?" the instructor asked from the chalkboard. "Don't worry about raising your hands, just shout it out." No one shouted out, nor did they raise their hand. Turning to the board, the instructor wrote a number for everyone to see: 100,212.

"Now," the instructor said, "does anyone know how many of these students are male?" Dead air again. Putting her hands on her hips, she said, "Come on, you can guess. Dare to be wrong. This isn't a test, this is a discussion."

A girl with brown pigtails said, "Two?"

"It's higher than that." The instructor turned back to the board and wrote a second number underneath the first: 6,008.

After marking down the number in her notes, Bridgett glanced to her right again. This time, she studied the blonde's face, a heart-shaped frame, containing the treasure of exquisite beauty. Slightly elevated cheekbones flanked a pair of blue eyes. The slight extension of her nose remained unblemished, even at its tip. Just below the blonde's nose lay a pair of moist, full lips painted an off-white color to match the girls around her.

Standing directly in front of Bridgett, the instructor asked, "Why do you think that number is so low?"

Bridgett quickly snapped her gaze back around and said, "The genome act?"

"Do you know what it's called?"

Bridgett shook her head, fighting the urge to only look to her right.

The instructor returned to the front of the room and said, "The genome act that—what's your name?"

"Bridgett."

"Right. The genome act Bridgett mentioned is called the Wenham-

Burton Act, and it is the most important piece of legislation written in the past hundred years. There isn't a single male in this class. About six percent of this student body is male. Over the entire population, males make up twelve percent. Where are the other six percent?"

***

At the end of class, Bridgett watched the blonde file out with several girls wearing similar skirts and blouses. The girl in black tapped Bridgett on the shoulder, distracting her again. "Find something you like?"

"No, Delilah," Bridgett said.

"Then why are you blushing?"

"I am not blushing."

"Right…"

Shaking her head, Bridgett said, "Let's get some lunch."

"Sure," Delilah said, "if you can stop blushing long enough to eat."

***

The cafeteria in the University Commons was the largest public eatery on campus. Its arched skylights illuminated and decorated the expansive room with natural light. The swarm of tables was broken by a single pathway leading from the entrance to the various food stations to an expanse of meeting rooms.

Bridgett sat only with Delilah, watching herds of young women shuffle single file toward fuller stomachs. The line marched in fractions throughout the cafeteria, crossing itself in increasingly intimate ways. A group of girls wearing blue t-shirts, blouses, or blazers drew Bridgett's attention, half of them having some blonde color to their hair.

Pushing a couple of potato chips into her mouth, Delilah asked, "You're looking for her again, aren't you?"

Bridgett turned, scanning over a different group of distant blondes. "Just a little."

"It's not just a little," Delilah said. "If you're sitting around somewhere, you're always looking for her."

"Not all the time," Bridgett said.

"Yes, you are. You keep watching entrances and hallways, not to mention every lounge you walk past. I thought I'd be nice and not say anything, but after three days, it's gotten ridiculous."

"Then what do you suggest?" Bridgett asked before taking a drink of soda.

"Do something. Don't just sit around waiting for her to walk by."

***

This page intentionally left blanket

ABOUT THE AUTHOR

Len Berry is a lover of anime, X-Men, and existential video games. As a Biology graduate from Southeast Missouri State University, he has a habit of reading about weird scientific discoveries. When he's not writing, Len is probably drawing weird worlds into existence, watching red panda videos, or contemplating too much philosophy.

Learn more about Len at **len-berry.com**